# Star-
## Spangled
# SUMMER

# By Ilene Cooper

---

## Books about <u>The Holiday Five</u>:

*Trick or Trouble?*

*The Worst Noel*

*Stupid Cupid*


## The <u>Hollywood Wars</u> series:

*My Co-Star, My Enemy*

*Lights, Camera, Attitude*

*Seeing Red*

*Trouble in Paradise*

THE HOLIDAY FIVE

Star-
Spangled
SUMMER

BY ILENE COOPER

VIKING

VIKING
Published by the Penguin Group
Penguin Books USA Inc., 375 Hudson Street, New York, New York 10014, U.S.A.
Penguin Books Ltd, 27 Wrights Lane, London W8 5TZ, England
Penguin Books Australia Ltd, Ringwood, Victoria, Australia
Penguin Books Canada Ltd, 10 Alcorn Avenue, Toronto, Ontario, Canada M4V 3B2
Penguin Books (N.Z.) Ltd, 182-190 Wairau Road, Auckland 10, New Zealand

Penguin Books Ltd, Registered Offices: Harmondsworth, Middlesex, England

First published in 1996 by Viking, a division of Penguin Books USA Inc.

1  3  5  7  9  10  8  6  4  2

LIBRARY OF CONGRESS CATALOGING-IN-PUBLICATION DATA
Cooper, Ilene.
Star spangled summer / by Ilene Cooper    p.    cm.—(The Holiday Five)
Summary : The Holiday Five's return to Camp Wildwood may be spoiled
when it appears that three of the girls may not be able to attend after all.
ISBN 0-670-85655-X
[1. Camps—Fiction.] I. Title. II. Series: Cooper, Ilene. Holiday Five.
PZ7.C7856Sp  1996  [Fic]—dc20    95-26458  CIP  AC

Printed in U.S.A.
Set in Century

*Star-Spangled* SUMMER

# ONE

"I can't wait!" Lia Greene stretched out on the plaid blanket and looked at her friends. "Only one more month, and then look out Camp Wildwood!"

"We're ba-a-ck!" Jill Lewis said with a grin.

Maddy Donaldson poked around the picnic basket and, in keeping with her diet, pulled out a peach. "I think we've done a pretty fine job of keeping our promise."

Kathy Wallace agreed. "The Holiday Five definitely lives. Don't you think, Erin?"

Last summer, the five bunkmates had vowed to stay in touch when camp was over. They had known it wouldn't be easy. They all lived in different suburbs surrounding Chicago, except for Erin Moriarity, who lived right in the city, so they couldn't see each other all the time. But Lia had come up with the idea of getting together on holidays, and it worked out great. Today, for instance, the Saturday of the Memorial Day weekend, they were spending at a picnic in Maple Park, where Lia lived.

"Erin?" Kathy looked at her curiously. "You're a million miles away."

"Oh, sorry." Erin looked back at her friends, with a guilty expression on her face. "I was just thinking about something else."

"What could be better than thinking about camp?" Lia asked.

"Unless she's thinking about Cal Bennett," Maddy said slyly. "How many times have you talked to him since the camp Christmas reunion?"

"A couple," Erin mumbled.

"Fourth of July," Jill said knowingly.

"Cal and Erin will be holding hands under the fireworks," Lia agreed.

Erin groaned. "That is such a stupid tradition."

"How can you say that?" Kathy asked. "It's been going on forever. It's probably in the camp manual." Kathy tried to make her voice sound official, but an occasional giggle escaped into her recitation: "Whoever holds hands under the Fourth of July fireworks at Camp Wildwood will be together for the rest of the summer."

"Well, it won't be Cal and me," Erin said. Silently, she added, *but right now, I don't want to tell you why.*

Maybe it was Erin's tone, but the mood shifted. "I don't know. It might be nice to have a boyfriend at camp," Lia said, looking up at the sky.

"What's happening with you and Scott?" Jill asked "I haven't heard any updates lately."

"He's going to camp in Wyoming. For the whole summer."

"Wyoming?" Kathy was surprised. "Almost everyone goes to camp around here. Wyoming's practically in another continent."

Lia watched the clouds go by. "It's some special riding camp. He started taking lessons a couple of months ago, and now he's totally into riding. So his mom found this place in Wyoming for him."

Maddy, who loved horses and riding herself, said enviously, "Wow, is he lucky."

"So you'd rather be with a bunch of horses than with us," Jill teased her.

Maddy looked confused for a minute, then got the

joke. "I guess I'd rather be with you guys," she said with a smile. "In Wyoming."

Now the girls were giggling again. They spent the rest of the afternoon playing volleyball, and then finally cleaning up their picnic so that they could get the trains that would take them home.

One thing that had helped the Holiday Five stay together was that the places they lived were all served by the same commuter train line, so they could get together without a lot of chauffering by parents. Lia was the most centrally located, in Maple Park. Maddy's stop was the northernmost station, Waukegan. Jill lived in Evanston, and Erin got off in Chicago, though she then had to take a bus to her house from the train station. Kathy's parents were divorced. She and her mother lived in the ritzy suburb of Lake Pointe; on weekends and on holidays, Kathy often stayed with her father and his new family, who had a high-rise apartment in Chicago. Today, she'd be taking the train all the way downtown with Erin.

Jill was on that train, too, at least as far as Evanston. As soon as they were settled, she looked at her watch and frowned.

"What's wrong?" Kathy asked her.

"I have to go to the rink and practice tonight, and I don't want to be late."

"On a Saturday night?" Erin asked with surprise.

"I promised my teacher I'd get some skating time in over the holiday, and this is my only chance."

Jill was a serious ice skater. She had won several competitions, and when the other girls had gone to watch her skate, they had all been impressed.

"Boy, what I want to do is take a nap," Kathy said. "That volleyball knocked me out."

"Well, I wouldn't mind taking a nap either," Jill said, "but none of the kids I'm skating against are going to be sleeping, so I better get on the ice."

After Jill got off, Kathy and Erin talked about Jill's skating. "I don't know how she does it," Kathy said. "I can barely manage to finish my homework, see my friends, and practice the piano—and I only do that when my mom gets on me."

Erin replied thoughtfully, "Jill's really into her skating. I guess when you love something that much, you make the time."

Anyone watching the girls as the train chugged its way downtown would have thought they made an odd-looking pair. Kathy, a tall brunette, had an air of so-

phistication that came from more than just wearing
the right clothes and having a sleek haircut. Erin, on
the other hand, was short and pixieish, but with a ve-
neer of toughness earned from being the second old-
est in a large family where money was usually in short
supply. Erin knew that if she wanted something, she'd
better be prepared to fight for it, because no one was
going to hand anything to her. Only once had she gotten something wonderful out of the blue, and that was
her scholarship last year to Camp Wildwood.

The girls parted at the train station. Kathy was
going to grab a cab to her father's house. Erin, of
course, would be taking the bus. She used to resent
Kathy for what seemed such an easy and affluent life.
But at Christmastime, Erin had learned that sometimes money wasn't enough to ensure happiness;
Kathy had run away from her own complicated family
situation to spend the holiday with the easygoing Moriaritys.

*Still,* Erin thought with a sigh, as she clambered
aboard the bus, *it would be nice not to have to
worry, for a change, about whether there was
going to be cash for any extras.* Actually, she didn't
have to worry about it. With six kids who all needed
and wanted things, there definitely wasn't going to be

enough money. There sure wasn't enough for Erin to spend a second summer at an expensive camp.

Looking out the dirty bus window, without seeing a thing, Erin thought how rotten she was going to feel when she finally made herself tell the rest of the girls she wouldn't be joining them in Bunk Three this year. She had vowed to herself that she would tell them at the picnic, but when the time had come, she just couldn't. Everyone was having such a good time, she didn't want to be the one to ruin the mood.

Besides, maybe something would happen to change the inevitable. Erin's natural optimism flickered for about a second. Then she thought, *Oh right. Let's see, a rich, and of course, long-lost relative could die and leave me money. Or I might find a million dollars in a paper sack on the Clark Street bus.* Yes indeed, the possibilities were endless.

By the time the bus arrived at her stop, Erin had talked herself into a very foul mood. She warned herself that she'd better not show it too much, though. Her family already thought that Erin often came back from her Holiday Five gatherings down because she didn't have the same lifestyle as the rest of the girls. She usually denied it because she didn't want them to know how right they were.

Kicking at a dented can on the sidewalk, Erin figured it didn't matter what her family thought anyway, because the good times were about to end. The girls would go to camp without her. There would be a new girl in their bunk, and in the fall, the Holiday Five would go on—she just wouldn't be one of them.

"Thank you," Kathy said politely as she tipped the cab driver. Then she pasted a smile on her face and took the elevator up to the nineteenth floor. You only have to stay until tomorrow, she reminded herself. Her mom was having a cookout tomorrow afternoon, so Kathy didn't have to spend the whole holiday weekend with her dad. There were plenty of rotten things about being the child of divorced parents, but being split down the middle for holidays was one of the things that bugged her the most.

Her father answered the door. "Hi, hon," he said, giving her a hug. "I was just starting to get worried about you."

Kathy looked around. The apartment seemed surprisingly empty. Dr. Wallace lived here with his second wife, Marion, their three-year-old daughter, Helena, and Marion's daughter, Anne, who was just a year older than Kathy. Whenever Kathy came over, she had to share a bedroom with Anne, an arrangement that didn't please either one of the girls.

"Where is everybody?"

"They went to the movies."

"Am I that late? You didn't say I should be here in time to catch a show."

"No, no. It came up at the last minute, and I told Marion to just go ahead. This gives me a little time to spend alone with you."

Kathy smiled at her dad. Ever since Christmas, he had been making a major effort to spend more time with her. Time alone, without Helena interrupting their conversations, or Marion asking her husband to do this or that.

"So what are we going to do with this time?" Kathy asked as she sat down carefully on the white sofa. Even though Helena could be a terror, Marion always managed to have the house looking as though it had just been straightened up for company. Kathy supposed that wasn't so odd, since Maria, the housekeeper, did show up almost every day.

"Marion's going to bring home some Chinese food after the movie, but maybe you're hungry now?"

Kathy shook her head. "The picnic filled me up. Erin made brownies, Lia brought potato chips, Mom was making banana bread for her cookout, so I brought that—"

"Didn't anyone eat real food?" Dr. Wallace interrupted with a frown.

"They were selling hot dogs at the park. We had those for a main course."

"That wasn't exactly what I meant," the doctor muttered. "So what else did you girls do?"

"We played volleyball. That knocked off a few of the calories," Kathy assured him. "And we talked."

"I'm sure. How do you kids find so much to talk about?" Dr. Wallace asked, shaking his head. "I swear, I think the phone here is permanently attached to Anne's ear."

"Then it's a good thing you're a surgeon," Kathy pointed out.

Dr. Wallace had to smile. "Do boys talk on the phone as much as girls? I never did."

Kathy had a hard time picturing her father as a kid. Not that she didn't know what he'd looked like. There were about a million photos of him hanging on her grandmother's wall. What he had been like was a different issue. Intense, a perfectionist, bossy sometimes, that's how she would describe her father. All those qualities, Kathy supposed, fit with his being a well-respected orthopedic surgeon. She didn't quite know how they translated into being a boy.

"The phone probably is a girl thing," Kathy admitted.

Dr. Wallace picked up his drink from the coffee table and began circling the rim of it with his forefinger. "It's quite something the way you stayed in touch with your camp friends all year. I suppose you're looking forward to going back this summer."

"Sure. We spent most of the afternoon talking about it."

"Are all the girls returning?"

Kathy nodded. She looked at her father suspiciously. This sounded like it was leading up to something.

"What if I asked you to change your plans? Would you be terribly upset?"

"Not go back to Camp Wildwood? Dad, you're kidding!"

"Well, it's not as if I'm asking you to stay home. I have something even better than camp in mind."

Kathy didn't say anything. She just waited, looking at Dr. Wallace through narrowed eyes.

"London. And Paris."

"What about them?"

"We're going, right after Anne is done with school for the year. We want you to come with us. Now, don't be shaking your head, Kathy, until you hear me out. Marion has let me know in no uncertain terms that I haven't been spending enough time with the family. Just like the way you let me know at Christmas."

"But Dad . . ."

"No. Let me finish. So, Marion and I planned the trip of a lifetime. One week in London, another in the English countryside. And then we wind up in Paris."

Kathy was horrified. "Dad, I don't want to go."

"You haven't even thought about it," Dr. Wallace snapped.

"I don't have to. Besides, Mom wants me to go to camp."

"I've talked to your mother. She said it's your decision to make. Whatever you want is all right with her."

Kathy got up and walked over to a wall of windows that looked out on Lincoln Park. London and Paris? They sounded fine. But she didn't want to traipse across Europe sharing a bedroom with Anne and feeling like a fifth wheel on the Wallace family caravan. Besides, her summer at camp was all planned. The girls had done everything this afternoon from choose the activities they wanted to participate in to speculate on which boys would be back at Wildwood.

"As I said, Kathy," Dr. Wallace continued, "it's your decision, but I want you to know, I'll be very disappointed if you don't join us."

Kathy sighed. She could take it when her father seemed distant from her or even when he was mad. But disappointed? That was the worst.

# Two

---

Erin kicked off the covers. Despite the fan blowing from the doorway, the small attic bedroom she shared with her older sister Maureen was hot. She turned her pillow trying to find a cool spot. If it was this uncomfortable in May, how was it going to be a month from now? Well, she'd find out, Erin thought bitterly, because stuck in this bedroom was where she was going to be.

When Erin turned over for the third time in five minutes, Maureen yawned and asked Erin, "What is your problem?"

"I feel like I'm in an oven."

"Go to sleep, and you won't know how hot it is," Maureen instructed.

"I'm not sleepy."

Maureen turned on the bedside lamp and sat up. "Well I guess that means I'm not going to sleep either. Do you want to talk?"

"About what?" Erin asked cautiously.

"How was your picnic with your friends?"

"It was okay."

"Just okay? Usually you're totally on the ceiling after one of your Holiday Five outings."

Maureen could be a pretty nice big sister, but she liked to push Erin's buttons sometimes, too. Maureen never had thought that going off to Camp Wildwood was such a good idea. "Are they all going back to camp this summer?" she asked.

"Yeah."

"I guess they feel bad you won't be with them."

Erin didn't answer.

"Erin, they do know that you're not going back, don't they?"

"Who says I'm not going back?"

Maureen looked at her sister as if she were crazy. "What are you talking about, Erin? Your scholarship from Family Services was for just one summer."

Erin pushed her sweaty bangs away from her forehead. "We don't exactly know that. I've never really

asked if they were offering the scholarships for another year."

"I don't think they'd give them to the same kids
even if they were."

"You don't know that," Erin said hotly. "You don't
know anything about how Family Services works."

"Keep your voice down!" Maureen hissed. "You're
going to wake the little kids."

"They probably can't sleep in this heat either," Erin
muttered.

"Listen, I'm sorry you can't go to camp, but you'd
better get over it. It's not going to happen. Good night,
Erin," Maureen said as she turned off the light.

There was nothing like being told she couldn't do
something to raise Erin's ire. So Maureen was sure
that she wasn't going to camp? Well, that was just another reason to find a way.

The next morning, Erin woke up early, though not
so early that her father hadn't already left for work.
Maureen was sleeping in, and it looked like the twins,
Tim and Pat, were also still asleep. But her seven-
year-old brother, Danny, was watching some show
about dinosaurs in the living room, and her mother
was feeding little Jeanette in the kitchen.

"Do you want me to finish, Mom?"

"Oh, would you?" Mrs. Moriarity asked gratefully. "I'd like to throw in another load of laundry."

Erin didn't mind watching her brothers and sister. It was kind of fun, actually. The twins were ten and didn't listen to her very much, but Danny was a good kid, and Jeanette adored her.

Jeanette was just learning to talk. As soon as Erin sat down across from her, she started, saying, "Rin, Rin," in a happy voice, which was the best she could do with Erin's name.

"Yes," Erin cooed back at her. "Erin's going to feed you breakfast."

"No!" That was Jeanette's latest word, and the one she seemed to like best. She knew what it meant, too, because Erin wasn't able to get one more spoonful of cereal down her. Finally, Erin sprung her sister from the high chair, and Jeanette crawled away into the living room, where Danny pulled her down beside him.

With Jeanette out of the way, Erin had some toast and juice, and then began to clean up the kitchen. All the kids were expected to pitch in, and by now it was habit. It was hard for her mother to keep on top of the chores, and no wonder. After first Maureen and then the twins wandered downstairs and had their breakfasts, it was time to clean everything up again.

Erin was taking a breather when her mother came upstairs with a pile of folded towels.

"Where is everyone?" she asked.

"Maureen went to her sitting job, and the twins are playing in the park. Danny and Jeanette are still watching TV.

Mrs. Moriarity sat down heavily and put her towels on the clean table. She reached over and touched Erin's hair. "And what are you going to do until it's time to go down to the beach?" The family had planned to spend the afternoon there after Mr. Moriarity got home. During the week, he worked as a foreman in a factory, and sometimes during the weekend he did body work at a local garage.

"I guess I can go see if Gina's home. Or maybe I'll just read."

Mrs. Moriarity got up and took her towels. "That sounds fine." She was headed for the stairway when Erin's voice stopped her.

"Mom, I want to go back to camp."

Her mother looked at her sadly. "I'm sure you do."

"There isn't any way we could swing it?" Erin hated, absolutely hated, asking, but she had to give it a shot.

"I don't see how. There are so many things we need.

The dryer's on the fritz, and a dishwasher would be wonderful. All the kids have things they want, Erin, you know that."

"I know. But Maureen went to St. Louis at spring break to visit Aunt Nina, and the twins and Danny are going to day camp."

"Erin, all those things together don't add up to what just the first session of your overnight camp would cost."

"Fine. Whatever." Erin got up and practically threw the milk carton into the refrigerator. When Erin turned around, her mother had taken the towels upstairs. *All right, I know where I stand now,* Erin told herself. A plan began to formulate in her mind, and Erin began to feel a little better knowing there was something else she could do to get herself to camp. She was impatient, but she knew she couldn't get started on phase two until Tuesday afternoon.


"Where are you going?"

Erin looked at her friend Gina and tried not to lie. "I've got an errand to run."

"Want me to go with you?" Gina asked as she swung on her backpack.

"Oh, that's okay. Maybe I'll call you when I get home."

Gina gave Erin a funny look, but she shrugged and said, "All right. We've got that history test to study for on Wednesday. Maybe we can get going on it tonight."

Erin was relieved once Gina turned off on her block. Going to Family Services and asking about the scholarship program was hard enough on her own. She didn't want to answer Gina's questions as well. Gina had already asked Erin if she wanted to start a play group for little kids over the summer so they could make some money. Erin had told her maybe.

As she turned down Division Street, Erin thought back to last summer when she had first learned she was going to Camp Wildwood. The whole thing had been something of a fluke.

Mrs. Moriarty had been down at the Family Services offices one afternoon picking up some Meals on Wheels forms for one of their housebound neighbors. She had spotted a poster advertising five scholarships to area overnight camps for Erin's age group, and while she was waiting, she applied for a camp scholarship. Then she had forgotten all about it.

Several weeks later, Mrs. Ogden at Family Services

had interrupted their dinner with the news that one of the scholarships belonged to Erin. Mrs. Moriarity had come back to the table in something of a daze.

"Erin, I have some good news for you, I think." Then she told Erin and the rest of the family the story.

When she looked back, it was funny to remember that at the time, she hadn't been at all pleased. "Who wants to go to overnight camp?" Erin had asked indignantly.

"Why should she go all the way to Wisconsin?" Mr. Moriarity added with a frown. "She has a perfectly good bed right here."

"But Joe," Mrs. Moriarity responded, "this is a wonderful opportunity. There's swimming up there, and riding, and all kinds of arts and crafts . . ."

"It's for the whole summer?" Pat asked.

When Mrs. Moriarity nodded, Maureen said happily, "I'd have the room to myself."

"Who said I was going, anyway?" Erin groused. Though she would not have admitted it for the world, this felt more like a punch in the stomach than a lucky break. She had never been much of anywhere, certainly not without her family. Camp was okay. She had been to the park district day camp for a couple of summers and had liked it. But leaving home? Meeting a strange bunch of kids? And for the whole summer? Erin's immediate thought was, *No way!*

But over the next couple of days, Mrs. Moriarity had several long talks with Erin about what a special opportunity this was.

"We could never afford to send you to a camp like this, Erin," Mrs. Moriarity told her one night as Erin was getting ready for bed. "Don't just say no because you're scared."

"Scared?" Erin bristled. She was considered the tough one in the family, the one who was never frightened of anything. She had assumed that if she turned down the scholarship, everyone would just think it was because she didn't want to go. She'd die if they thought she'd turned it down because she was afraid.

Finally, she had agreed to go to Camp Wildwood. The first couple of days were even worse than she'd imagined. She'd arrived with all her stuff in a cardboard box, unaware that trunks were the proper way to transport things. And her bunkmates! What a bunch of stuck-up snobs. At least, that's what Erin had thought at first. It took four days for her to realize that she was feeling left out because Maddy, Jill, Kathy, and Lia had all met the summer before. It wasn't until they all sneaked out together for a night-time swim that Erin actually felt like one of the gang.

Now, she couldn't imagine wanting anything more than she wanted to go back to camp. With determination, she pushed open the door of the Family Services office.

"Is Mrs. Ogden here?" Erin asked the young woman at the front desk.

"Do you have an appointment?" the woman responded.

Erin shook her head.

"Well, then, I'm sorry . . ."

"It's really important."

The woman checked the appointment book. "Mrs. Ogden has a full schedule this afternoon."

Catching sight of Erin's disappointed face, the receptionist said, "I guess I can ask her if she has a moment before her next appointment comes in. Give me your name."

Erin went to sit down and wait, but before she had even picked up a magazine, she was being beckoned by Mrs. Ogden into her office.

"Hello, Erin," Mrs. Ogden said, escorting her to a chair inside the office. "It's been a long time since I've seen you."

Erin wondered if perhaps she should have kept in touch with Mrs. Ogden. Maybe her chances for a scholarship would have been better, but it had never crossed her mind. "I've been busy," Erin replied lamely.

Mrs. Ogden, a crisp woman in her fifties, nodded. "I'm sure you have. I trust you kept your grades up this year."

Erin nodded. Her good grades were one of the reasons she had been given the scholarship in the first place. "I was on the Honor Roll."

"Excellent," Mrs. Ogden said, as she leaned against her desk. "Now, what can I do for you? As Shelly told you, I don't have much time today."

Taking a deep breath, Erin said, "I'd like to go back to camp, Mrs. Ogden. It would really mean a lot to me."

For a moment, Mrs. Ogden looked confused. Then she said gently, "But Erin, we're not awarding scholarships this year."

"None at all?" Erin asked with disappointment.

"Our funding has been slashed. We have to use our money for the really important things like the Meals on Wheels program and our day-care center." Looking at Erin's crestfallen face, Mrs. Ogden said, "I'm sorry.

We had a budget surplus last year, and that's how the camp program came about. Perhaps some other year, we'll be able to do it again."

Who cared if the camp scholarships would be instituted again at some later date? It was this summer Erin wanted to go. She stood up. "Well, thank you anyway, Mrs. Ogden."

"At least you got to enjoy camp for one year," Mrs. Ogden said patting her on the shoulder.

*Oh, a fat lot of good that did,* Erin thought belligerently as she headed home. Didn't those social services agencies ever think? They got your hopes up by letting you do something wonderful like go to camp, and then they say no more money, forget about it, you can't do it ever again. Maybe Maureen was right. Maybe it would have been better if she had never gone to camp at all. At least she wouldn't be hurting so much right now.

Erin moped her way through dinner, but she didn't care. As Pat and Tim teased Mr. Moriarity about buying his weekly lottery ticket, Erin just pushed her food around on the plate.

"You should use Michael Jordan's birth date for the numbers," Tim informed his dad. "They would be lucky for sure."

Pat took a bite of his spaghetti. "Our birthdays never win anything."

Mr. Moriarity shook his head. "No, my family's my luck, and that's why I play the numbers in your birthdays. Someday I'll win."

Erin just kept eating. *I won't hold my breath,* she thought.

When the phone rang, Mrs. Moriarity, who was about to serve dessert, answered it. The kids weren't allowed to have phone calls during dinner, but Mrs. Moriarity, perhaps hoping the call would cheer Erin up, handed her the phone.

It was Cal. Normally Erin loved hearing from him, but today he was the last person she wanted to talk to.

Cal, however, didn't pick up on this. At least not immediately.

"Erin, do you know what today is?"

"No."

"In exactly one month, we'll be at camp."

Erin didn't say anything.

"It's going to be so great. I mean, I like everything about camp, but seeing you, well, that's right up there. Erin," Cal said hesitantly, "there was something I wanted to ask you."

"What's that?" Erin asked through tight lips.

"You're going to watch the fireworks with me on the Fourth, aren't you?"

There was that stupid tradition again. Erin felt all the anger she had about missing camp whipping around inside her. Some of it spilled over on Cal. "No. No, I'm not."

"What do you *mean?*"

"Because I'm not going back to camp. I guess you forgot, I was there on scholarship," Erin said roughly. "Well, there's no more money for me to go back."

Cal stumbled all over his words. "I'm sorry. I didn't know."

"Yeah, so have a great time at camp. I'm sure after a couple of days you won't even know I'm not there." Without even a good-bye, Erin hung up.

The Moriarity house was too small for secrets. When Erin walked back into the dining room, tears stinging her eyes, everyone was looking at her. Even Jeanette's eyes were wide.

This made Erin even madder.

"What's everyone staring at? Didn't you know how much I wanted to go to camp?" Erin cried. "Instead, I'm going to be stuck with all of you this summer. Won't that be fun."

# THREE

Jill took one more turn around the rink, did one more jump, and then skated off toward the bleachers, where her teacher was waiting.

Tony Fortunato had been Jill's skating instructor since she began her lessons, four years ago. Even though she had only been eight, that was considered late to begin skating, especially if you had any serious ambition.

Of course, when Jill started she had only wanted to skate for fun. She remembered clearly the time she first started paying any attention to skating at all. It was during the 1988 Winter Olympics. Debi Thomas, who was skating for the United States, was an African American like Jill, and that caught her attention. But it took another Olympics before Jill started asking if she could be a skater, and finally her parents agreed she could have lessons on a trial basis. Evanston, where she lived, had a very nice facility, and Tony immediately recognized Jill as a student with potential. It wasn't long before skating became more than just an after-school activity.

Still, it was only in the last year or so that Jill had begun to compete seriously. Tony had thought it was best to ease her into that world. After a few small meets, she had gone on to win a regional competition for twelve and unders during spring break. That had been a truly wonderful moment. Standing in the center of the ice, a stadium full of fans cheering her, Jill knew the excitement and pride she was feeling were the same emotions her heroines and heroes had when they won a major skating competition. It was a feeling she didn't want to let go of.

The win seemed to change things for Jill. Even though she knew that getting to the top of the skating world was a rough, expensive climb, Jill began to dream big dreams. If she kept improving and winning meets, maybe one day it would be Jill Lewis going for the gold. It was sure fun to think about.

"Not too bad," Tony commented, as Jill began un-lacing her skates.

Jill grimaced. Her toes hurt. It seemed like her feet were growing faster than any other part of her. She probably needed a new pair of skates. Between lessons and rink time and equipment, Jill knew that her parents put a lot of money into her hobby.

"But you've still got a long way to go on your axels," Tony continued.

Jill nodded. Axels were a tricky maneuver that meant making one and a half revolutions in the air. She'd just have to practice harder. "Maybe I can spend time on that tomorrow." She had planned to skip practice tomorrow for a shopping trip with her friends, but she supposed that now she'd have to reconsider the outing.

"By the way," Tony said, pulling a brochure out of his pocket. "I found this when I was cleaning out my in box yesterday."

"It's for a skating camp," Jill said, looking it over. There was an impressive picture of a couple twirling around the ice on the cover.

"It's late to sign up, but I know the owner. I could probably get you in."

"But I'm already going to overnight camp. Camp Wildwood," Jill said, looking troubled.

"It's only a thought. A way to keep practicing over the summer." Tony got up. "You'll have to talk to your parents about whether it's feasible to change your plans."

Wiping her brow with her towel, Jill sat on the bench and looked over the brochure with interest. The camp sounded intense. Although there were other activities, most of the day was spent skating on a well-equipped rink. Jill felt a flutter of excitement. Going to this camp could be great. The other counselors were top-notch, and the other campers were sure to be good, too. She could learn a lot there, she was certain.

But as she was showering and changing back to her street clothes, Jill began to think about what she'd have to give up for skating camp—Camp Wildwood, the Holiday Five, and all their plans. Is that really what she wanted to do?

She remembered the day she had won the regionals. Tony had asked, "How far do you want to go with this, Jill?" and in the flush of first place, she'd replied, "All the way! To the Olympics!"

Tony had given her a funny look. "That's a lofty

goal," he'd said. *Would going to skating camp make it a more reachable one?* Jill wondered.

As usual after a late-afternoon practice, Jill's dad was waiting to pick her up. He was a schoolteacher at a suburban high school, and he was often home before Jill's mother, who worked part-time as a nurse.

"How are you, baby?" Mr. Lewis asked as Jill slid into the passenger side of the car.

"Tired." Jill yawned. "Exhausted."

"Too tired to go out to eat?"

"Out to eat?" She had been looking forward to a warm, relaxing bubble bath. Do we have to?" she asked.

"Well, your mama's waiting at the restaurant. Mario's."

Jill shrugged. She loved their lasagna. "Is Owen going with us?"

"You know your brother. Since he started high school, he thinks going out with his family is about the most embarrassing thing that could happen to him. He said he'd grab something at home."

Mario's was not one of those hip, new places with lots of wood beams and soft lighting. It had looked the same for as long as Jill could remember, and her parents said it remained unchanged from a couple of decades before that. The wallpaper was gold with red flocking and the tables and chairs were big and heavy and made out of dark wood. You came to Mario's when you wanted food, and a lot of it.

Jill's mother wasn't at the restaurant as they thought she'd be by the time Mr. Lewis and Jill got there, but they allowed themselves to be seated anyway. While they were still reading the menu, she arrived, slightly out of breath from rushing.

"Whew. I thought I'd never get out of that hospital."

"Was something wrong with one of the babies?" Jill asked with concern. Her mother worked on the neonatal floor of the hospital with the newborns.

"No, nothing wrong. Three of them just decided to make their entrances at the same time."

"What did their parents name them?" Jill asked. She was fascinated by the names parents gave their infants.

"The little girl was Keenisha, and the boys were Reed and Jack."

"The girls always have the most interesting names." Jill loved little babies and wanted to begin babysitting, but there never seemed to be any time for that.

"How was the skating today?" Mrs. Lewis asked as she scanned the menu.

Jill had been itching to bring out the brochure about skating camp, but she'd wanted to wait until her mother had arrived and was settled in. "Tony gave me this," she said, pulling the now slightly crumpled flyer from her pocket.

While her parents were looking it over, Jill said, "Tony just found out about it. He said even though it's late, he can get me in."

"Is that what you want?" Mr. Lewis asked with a frown. "I thought you were all excited about going back to Camp Wildwood."

"Where we've already put down a deposit," Mrs. Lewis added.

Jill wavered. Skating camp might be great for her future glory, but going back to Camp Wildwood with the Holiday Five had been the pot of gold after a long, work-filled year. Maybe her parents would make the decision for her. "I guess I'd better forget it?" Jill asked.

"No one said that," Mr. Lewis replied. "But this is coming out of the blue. I thought you wanted to play this summer." He flipped through the flyer. "This isn't going to be playtime."

"It seemed like a good opportunity," Jill said. She knew her parents were big on good opportunities.

Her mother and father exchanged glances. "I guess we can think about it," Mrs. Lewis finally said.

"If all this skating is what you really want." Her father gave her a serious look. "Is it, baby?"

"Well, sure," Jill said, but she was starting to realize what kind of summer she was letting herself in for.

After the waiter took their order, Mrs. Lewis said, "Jill, where do you see yourself going with all this skating, anyway?"

Now that was a question she could answer. "To the Olympics," Jill said dreamily.

"The Olympics!"

Her mother's tone brought Jill up short. She'd almost forgotten that all the television interviews, cheers from the crowd, the presentation of the medal had been going on strictly in her head.

"It could happen," she said. Her defiant tone was mostly to mask her embarrassment.

"*Could* isn't the same as *will*," Mr. Lewis murmured.

"Daddy," Jill said with outrage, "don't you have any faith in me?" If her parents had doubts, well, then, Jill was going to prove she had none.

"It's not a matter of faith, baby, it's a matter of numbers. Do you know how many kids want to win that medal? Thousands of them probably, and there's only one gold medal."

"So?"

"So, it takes big money to finance that kind of skating career," Mrs. Lewis told her. "It's one thing to send you to skating camp. It's another to get you to the Olympics."

Jill didn't say anything. Instead, she dug into her pasta. This camp business was getting her all confused. She wanted to forget it all and just enjoy her food.

Her parents must have sensed her mood, or maybe they just wanted a relaxing meal, too. In any case, no one talked anymore about camp until her parents were drinking their coffee. Then her father said, "Jill, I want you to take some time and really look at this camp thing from all the angles."

"I don't have that much time—" Jill began, but Mr. Lewis cut her off with a wave of his hand.

"You've got a little while. And while you're at it, baby, decide how much of yourself you want to put into skating, too. Are you really ready to make such a big commitment? I thought you were skating because you liked it so much. That's a lot different from spending every minute skating so you can get into Olympic competition."

By the time Jill arrived home, the lasagna she had eaten was sitting in her stomach like a stone. Owen was lying on the living room couch, his Walkman plugged into his ears. Jill was sure he was listening to the hip-hop music he loved so much. He opened one eye when Jill sank into the chair across from him.

"What's happening?" he asked.

Jill made a motion for him to turn off the music. Owen could be a pain, but sometimes he was easier to talk to than her parents. Quickly, she filled him in on her new option for the summer.

Her brother looked surprised. "I thought you were all set to go to Weirdwood." For some reason, Owen always thought that was a funny nickname for the camp.

"I was. Now I'm thinking that spending my summer skating is a better use of my time."

Owen snorted. "This is not a big problem, sister. Go where you'll have the most fun."

"It's not just about fun," Jill muttered. That was the last thing it was about.

She could see that Owen was the wrong one to be

having this conversation with. Suddenly, it was clear who the right person would be. Without another word to Owen, Jill went upstairs. She took the portable phone out of its home on the hall table, went into her room, and shut the door behind her.

Before she made her call, Jill looked around her room. Everywhere she looked, there were things to remind her that skating was the number-one thing in her life. Posters of Debi Thomas and other great skaters like Katarina Witt and Oksana Bayul took up most of the space on her walls. Across from her bed, her dad had made a special shelf to hold her regional trophy, which was surrounded by photographs of her at various skating events. Even most of the books that lined her bookshelf had something to do with the sport.

Flopping down on her bed, Jill found it easy to drift off again to that sunny world where everything worked out just the way you wanted it to. She thought about the acclaim a champion skater received. Nancy Kerrigan had gotten to ride in a big parade at Disney World after she won the silver medal in the last Olympics. A parade would be fun, Jill thought. Maybe she'd wear a long dress in pink. Pink was her favorite color. She'd carry pink roses, too.

Jill was roused from her reverie by the phone ringing in her hand. Its shrill sound almost scared her. "Boy, this must be telepathy," Jill told Lia. "I was just about to call you."

"Did you hear about Kathy, too?" Lia asked.

"Kathy? What's with her?"

Lia filled Jill in on Dr. Wallace's request for a change in the summer plans.

"That's awful!" Jill said automatically. Then she realized Kathy's dad was not the only one fouling up the Holiday Five's plans. "But Lia, I've got something to tell you, too."

Lia didn't like Jill's tone. "What's wrong?"

Jill took a deep breath and told her all that had happened in the last couple of hours.

"Oh, swell," Lia said mournfully. "Just last Saturday we were planning what a great time we were going to have at camp. Now it looks like Hello Summer, Goodbye Holiday Five."

# FOUR

Visiting Kathy's house always gave Erin a jolt. It was hard to believe that a real person lived here, much less a real person that she actually knew.

"This is some place," Mr. Moriarity said, as he pulled into the long driveway edged with tulips and irises on either side. "And only Kathy and her mother live here?"

"And the housekeeper."

"The housekeeper," Mr. Moriarity said, as if he couldn't quite fit the word with a mental picture.

"If you think the outside is nice, you should see the inside. And there's a tennis court out back."

Mr. Moriarity just shook his head.

Erin looked at her dad and felt a rush of love for

him. Maybe their house wasn't the biggest or the best, but no one worked harder than Joe Moriarity to provide for his family, and no one wanted more to have his family happy.

"What time should I pick you up?" he asked Erin.

"Dad, I told you you didn't have to wait. I can take the train back."

"No, I've got a few errands that I can do up here. How about I pick you up in two hours?"

"All right," Erin agreed.

Mr. Moriarity flashed her a smile. "And I'll buy my lottery ticket here. Just for a change of pace. Could be lucky."

It was tradition with Mr. Moriarity to buy his one lottery ticket every Saturday, using various combinations of his children's birthdays. Not that they had proved terribly lucky so far.

"Okay, Pop. I'll be right back out here in two hours."

Erin was rather surprised to find herself at Kathy's this Saturday morning. She hadn't been expecting to see her friends so soon. But Lia had telephoned last night to tell her that an emergency meeting of the Holiday Five had been called. Erin hadn't been home at the time, and Danny had gotten the message all garbled, but apparently something was up with Kathy and Jill.

Mrs. Curtis, the housekeeper, let Erin into the house.

"The girls are in Kathy's room. You know where it is. Upstairs and to the right."

Erin thanked her, passed the family room, with its big stone fireplace, and then climbed the stairs to Kathy's room.

The girls were scattered around the room—Kathy and Lia on the bed, Jill on the floor next to them, and Maddy stretched out on the chaise longue. Erin dropped down and joined Jill.

"Hi, guys. So what's going on?" Erin asked.

Kathy looked the most upset. "I was just telling everyone. My father wants me to go to Europe with him and his family." Kathy made a face. Everyone knew what she thought of Dr. Wallace's brood.

"And there's more bad news," Maddy added.

"Not exactly bad," Jill murmured. "My coach told me about a skating camp in Indiana, and I'm thinking of going."

Erin was stunned. So she wasn't the only one who was having trouble finding her way back to Wildwood.

She knew that this was the perfect moment to say, "Hey, guess what? I can't go either." But something held her back. Her situation was very different from that of her friends. A trip to Europe? A fancy skating camp? What was so bad about those alternatives? Sure, they all wanted to return to Camp Wildwood, but if Kathy and Jill couldn't go, it wouldn't be like they were going to be stuck at home babysitting. No, that was Erin's fate alone.

Instead of a rush of sympathy for her friends, Erin could feel herself growing angry.

"Have you told your father you just don't want to go?" Maddy asked Kathy.

"Not exactly," Kathy replied. "He thinks he's making this fantastic effort to do the family thing. After all, I've been telling him I want to spend more time with him."

"But that's just it," Lia interrupted. "You meant with him. Not his wife, not Anne, not Helena."

Kathy sighed. "I don't think he knows the difference. He really wants us to be one big family."

"So what are you going to do?" Maddy asked.

"I don't know. That's why I wanted you guys to come over, so you could give me some ideas. Then Lia told me about Jill."

The girls turned to look at Jill, who was looking almost as upset as Kathy.

"I know you guys think I'm copping out on you. I really do want to go back to Wildwood. But if I'm ever going to get anywhere with my skating, I really should go to this camp."

Lia stretched a little on the bed. "There's two different things going on here. Kathy, you don't want to go to Europe." She turned to Jill. "You aren't sure how you feel about skating camp."

"That's what's making me crazy," Jill said. She'd done nothing but go over her options for the last couple of days.

"Well, which do you want to do more?" Kathy asked.

"I love skating, you all know that. And lately I've been getting good. But to get to be one of the best, well, that takes up just about your whole life."

"You take lessons a couple of times a week, don't you?" Erin asked.

Jill nodded. "And I practice even more. But you have no idea how much more I'd have to push myself to get good enough for regular competitions."

Maddy, who was not known for her love of exercise, except when she was riding a horse, made a face. "Sounds like a lot of trouble to me."

"Oh, it would be a lot of trouble . . . and sweat and effort and disappointment," Jill added. "Every athlete who's any good will tell you it takes all that and more to get somewhere."

"And do you want to get somewhere?" Lia asked gently.

"And where's somewhere, anyway?" Kathy added more bluntly. "I mean, do you want to be in the Olympics? The Ice Follies? What?"

A picture of herself with that gold medal flashed through Jill's mind, but she had already gotten burned when she mentioned the Olympics to her parents. That vision of victory wasn't for public consumption. It was more for imagining in the privacy of your bedroom.

"Wouldn't you get bored doing just one thing all the time?" Lia asked. "And what if you weren't going to be a famous skater? How would you feel then?"

Jill knew her friends were just trying to help, but their questions were making her more confused than ever. "I don't know." She shrugged helplessly. "I'm good. But am I that good?"

None of the girls knew the answer to that. Finally, Kathy said, "Maybe you should talk to someone who does know. Like that coach of yours."

Jill nodded. She hadn't really talked to Tony about skating camp since he'd given her the flyer. He'd acted as if he'd completely forgotten about it.

"You've got to figure out what you want to do," Lia finally said. "And not just about camp."

"My father said that, too." And that was the scary part, Jill thought.

"I think Kathy's problem is a lot easier to solve than Jill's," Maddy said from the chaise. "Kathy, just tell your dad you're not going."

"You don't know my dad." She got off the bed. "Why don't we continue this discussion downstairs? Worrying makes me really hungry, and I think there's some cookies down there."

The girls willingly followed Kathy downstairs and helped her bring cookies, lemonade, and some chips out to the backyard. Erin, who was still feeling sulky, looked around. The last time she had been to Kathy's house was in the middle of winter, and even with a blanket of snow, the grounds had been spectacular. But now, with all the spring flowers, and the trees bursting with pink and white blossoms, the whole yard looked like something off the cover of a house-and-garden magazine. Erin could feel the knot in her stomach growing. What did Kathy do to deserve all this?

As the girls began to discuss Kathy's situation once more, Erin thought to herself, *No one's ever asked whether going to camp this summer is going to be a problem for me.* Didn't they wonder where the money was coming from? *Everyone's so concerned about Kathy and Jill, didn't they think I could use a little of those feelings?*

She barely heard Lia saying, "I don't know what we'll do if you guys don't come to camp."

Maddy broke a cookie in half and asked, "What will happen to the Holiday Five if you're not there?"

"There won't be any Holiday Five," Kathy responded glumly.

"Hey, we can always still get together during the year," Lia said.

But each of the girls had her own doubts about that. It had taken a lot of effort to make time for each other in the midst of their regular lives. Would they even want to make that effort without the camp experience to bind them?

They sat quietly for a few minutes, then Maddy said, "Let's not talk about this anymore, okay? At least for a little while. We've gone over and over it, and we haven't come to any decisions."

"Maddy's right," Jill said, nodding. "We've worn

this out." She turned to Lia. "So do you and Scott have any plans for a big good-bye?"

"Oh no you don't," Lia said with a small smile. "Just because we're not going to talk about you anymore, doesn't mean we have to talk about me and Scott."

The bantering went on for a while, pure Holiday Five teasing. Erin, who was still mad but didn't want the others to question her, joined in just enough so that it wouldn't seem as if she was pouting.

The girls went on like that for a while, until Lia looked at her watch. "Oops. I've got to go. My mother's picking me up at the Maple Park station. If I miss my train, she'll kill me."

"And my mom should be coming any minute." Maddy got up out of her deck chair.

"I guess I'm taking the train with you, Lia," Jill said.

"What about you, Erin?" Kathy asked.

"My father's picking me up here, but not for about twenty minutes or so."

"That's okay," Kathy told her. "I'm not going anywhere. We can just hang until then."

After the others left, Kathy said, picking up the leftovers, "Why don't we go in? It's getting hot."

"All right," Erin said listlessly. She didn't want to be here anymore, inside or out; all the fanciness was getting on her nerves. But there was nothing to do but make the best of it until her father arrived.

"Oh, that reminds me," Kathy said as they entered the house, "I have some things from last summer that are way too small on me. Do you want to try them on? They'd be great for you to take to camp."

Erin didn't know what to say. Last winter, Kathy had given her an outfit that was the pride of the Moriarity closet. Both she and Maureen wore the sweater and skirt. At the time, Erin had been thrilled, but today, taking Kathy's hand-me-downs made her feel even more like a poor relation. Still, she didn't see how she could just rudely say no. Kathy was trying to be nice. It put Erin in a worse mood than ever.

"I guess." Erin practically stomped up the stairs behind Kathy.

Kathy went over to her dresser and pulled out a drawer. "Anything in here can go," she said casually.

Erin went over and looked at the pile of T-shirts and shorts. There was enough to outfit Erin for several summers.

"Why don't you start trying on? Then we can have a fashion show," Kathy said with a smile. "I think I'll run down and get some more lemonade. All that talking made me thirsty. Want some?"

Erin shook her head. When Kathy left, Erin, with a sigh, started pulling clothes out of the drawer. She threw a couple of shirts on the bed and was startled by the sound of a clink on the wood floor.

Leaning down, Erin picked up a pearl bracelet with a gold clasp. As she turned it around in her hand, she could see that this was no piece of costume jewelry. The clasp was too delicate, and the pearls had a pinkish gleam that made them look very expensive.

Wasn't that just like Kathy, Erin thought to herself. A valuable piece of jewelry, an heirloom probably, and Kathy had just tossed it in a drawer with clothes she wanted to give away. Or maybe she had left the bracelet in a pocket and hadn't even missed it for almost a year. It was a good thing Kathy hadn't just shoved these clothes in a Goodwill bag. She would never have gotten the bracelet back.

And then Erin had a thought. Why should she return this bracelet to Kathy? Obviously it didn't mean much to her. All the ugly feelings Erin had been having about her friends crystallized around the bracelet. Shouldn't she, Erin, have something pretty for a change? Something valuable even? Yes, she should. And what could be more perfect than this? A piece of jewelry that Kathy hadn't seen in so long she must have forgotten about it.

"So did the clothes fit?" Kathy asked as she came back into the room carrying her lemonade.

Quickly, Erin shoved the bracelet into her pocket. I . . . I've just started sorting through them."

Kathy picked up a red striped tee. "I like this one. I think it would look adorable with your hair."

Erin tried to put the bracelet out of her mind. She concentrated on the shirt. "Yes, let me try it." Feeling both guilty and oddly exhilarated, Erin took a few articles of clothing, without even paying much attention to what they were. When she heard her father honk, she grabbed them and practically flew down the stairs, with barely a good-bye and thanks to Kathy. Out of breath, she slid into the passenger's side and slammed the door of the car. "Let's go," Erin said.

Mr. Moriarity laughed. "You sound like a bank robber after a heist."

All the way home, the bracelet burned a hole in her pocket.

# FIVE

Kathy plunked her bag down in Anne's bedroom, knowing that in about three seconds, her stepsister would say, "Can't you put that in the closet?"

"Can't you put that in the closet?" Anne asked without even looking up from her *YM* magazine.

"Thank you."

"What for?" Anne asked.

"I just won a million-dollar bet with myself."

"Mmmm." Anne continued lying on her bed and leafing through her magazine.

Kathy ignored the bag, but did hang up her sweater. To her surprise, when she turned around, Anne had pushed the magazine aside and was looking at her.

"What?" Kathy asked. "Do I have a rip in my blouse or something?"

"I was just wondering what you decided about Europe."

Kathy wasn't sure what kind of a response Anne wanted. "It's not exactly my decision to make," she replied slowly.

"Your father didn't say you had to go, did he?"

"Not exactly. But you know how he can be. If you don't do what he wants, he acts like you took his favorite toy away from him."

Anne nodded, and it occurred to Kathy that Anne probably knew her father and his habits a lot better than she did. After all, she was the one who saw him every day.

"Well, I don't want to go on this trip either," Anne said, swinging her legs off the bed.

"You don't?" Here was an unexpected ally.

"I want to stay here. I was going to Great America, and Taste of Chicago is over the Fourth of July. I don't want to miss any of it."

Kathy thought, *Translate: She just wants to hang with her friends.* "Have you told your mother that?"

"No," Anne said, suddenly deflated. "I thought I should talk to them both, and I haven't been able to get them together. Not when they've both been in a good mood, anyway."

"Well, maybe you and I should talk to them." Kathy tried to remember if she and Anne had ever presented a united front on anything. She didn't think so, but who was to say there couldn't be a first time?

Anne looked skeptical at first; then she said, "I suppose we could try."

They waited until Helena had gone to bed that night. There was no use trying to discuss anything serious when their little sister was around. Helena seemed to have an uncanny sense about when the attention in the room was directed somewhere other than on herself. Then she would burst into the Barney song—or burst into tears.

Once Helena was safely tucked in, Anne said in her most authoritative about-to-be-high-school-freshman voice, "Mom, Elliot, we need to talk with you."

Dr. Wallace and his wife looked at each other. "All right," Marion finally said. "Let's go into the living room and talk."

When they were settled, Dr. and Mrs. Wallace looked at the girls expectantly. Anne, who had been so bold a moment before, said, "Go ahead, Kathy."

*Oh, thanks a lot,* Kathy thought, but she cleared her throat and said, "Dad, I think you know that I want to spend the summer at camp. Well, it turns out that Anne wants to stay home with her friends."

"You mean neither one of you wants to go on our trip?" Marion broke in, looking angry. "I have to tell you girls, that's so ungrateful."

Anne gave Kathy a look that said, *You messed up.* "It's not that we don't appreciate everything you want to do for us," Anne said smoothly. "London, Paris, who wouldn't want to go on a trip like that?"

"Who indeed," Marion said, slightly mollified.

"But both of us have already made so many wonderful plans," Anne continued.

Kathy thought Anne was laying it on a little thick. However, when she looked over at her dad and Marion, Marion, at least, seemed to be responding to Anne. "I suppose it *is* hard to leave your friends," Marion allowed.

"You did kind of spring this on us," Anne continued delicately.

Dr. Wallace, however, wasn't so easily swayed. "Can't we ever do anything as a family around here?" he asked grumpily.

"Elliot, we want to go to Europe, right, Kathy?" Anne didn't wait for Kathy to do more than nod her head. "We just wish it didn't have to be now."

Kathy had to give her stepsister credit. As she continued talking, clearly Anne was getting her father and Marion to listen. She made an eloquent plea about how important this last summer before high school was to her, ending by saying, "Next summer, I'll probably be working, and I won't have much free time at all."

Kathy doubted that, but she was even more surprised when Anne went on to talk about how much camp meant to Kathy. "Look how she's kept up with all her friends from Wildwood," Anne continued. "That took so much effort. If Kathy doesn't go back to camp, she probably won't even see them anymore."

Now Kathy almost laughed out loud. Anne had always told Kathy that getting together with her camp friends on holidays was totally dopey. But as she continued, it was clear Anne was making an impression.

"Perhaps the end of the summer might be a better time to go," Marion said, looking at her husband.

Dr. Wallace sighed. "I guess the reservations can be changed. You'll have to call the travel agent tomorrow, Marion."

"Really?" Anne squealed.

"You really ought to think about going into law, Anne," Dr. Wallace said. "You're quite a negotiator."

Kathy thought she ought to consider the theater. What an actress!

Anne got up and gave both her mother and her stepfather a kiss. "Thank you, thank you."

Kathy's relief at having the summer situation resolved was mixed with quite a bit of jealousy. While she was pleased that Europe was postponed and that camp was back in the picture, Kathy had to admit that it was Anne who had come through. She hadn't made the least bit of headway when she had talked to her dad alone.

As Anne walked back to her room, she whispered to Kathy, "Done. No thanks to you."

Kathy didn't even bother to answer back. Anne had the situation pegged. Nor did she want to join Anne in "their" room at the moment. Glumly, Kathy wondered what she should do with herself next. She always felt like a bird with no place to light when she was visiting her father. Finally, she wandered into the den, where Dr. Wallace was leafing through the *TV Guide*.

"Want to go outside?" she asked.

Her dad frowned. "What for?"

"For a walk."

Dr. Wallace looked as if he was fighting the urge to get comfortable on the couch and turn on some baseball. But he smiled at her gamely, and said, "Sure, let's walk along the lake."

Even though it was almost eight o'clock, it was still light out. Dr. Wallace nodded to the doorman as he and Kathy went outside. They crossed the busy street and made their way through the park area to the cement boardwalk, which was crowded, even at that hour, with Rollerbladers, bikers, and runners. It seemed as if Kathy and her dad were the only ones out for a simple stroll.

"I guess you're really glad to be going back to camp," Dr. Wallace said.

Kathy nodded.

"But?"

"But what?"

"There's something else. It's written all over your face."

Kathy moved a little closer to her dad to get out of a skater's way. She liked walking alongside him. It was easier to tell him things when she didn't have to look him in the eye. "I . . . I was just surprised at how easy it was for Anne to convince you to change the plans. I didn't get very far," Kathy added quietly.

Dr. Wallace seemed surprised. "Kathy, I was taking your wishes into account, too. When Anne said she didn't want to go, there didn't seem any point in pushing it."

Kathy didn't say anything.

"You know, I only planned this trip because I wanted us to do something big as a family. At Christmastime, you said you felt left out, that I didn't pay enough attention to you. Well, I've tried to do better, and then I got the idea for the trip." He was beginning to sound exasperated. "I'm not sure what you want."

What could Kathy say? That even now, years after the divorce, what she wanted was for her parents to get back together? There wasn't even the slimmest prayer of that happening, and Kathy knew it. Finally, she murmured, "Dad, I know you'd like it to happen, but I don't think we're ever all going to be one big happy family."

"Why shouldn't we?"

Kathy kicked at a stone. "Because Anne and I don't like each other, and because Marion's not my mom, and because I only see you every other weekend." There, she'd finally said it.

Dr. Wallace didn't say anything for a long time. When he did, it was only "Oh."

Now she did look up at her father. "Sorry, Daddy."

He put his arm around her, but he didn't say anything else. They just walked for a while, and then turned around and went back to the apartment.

Kathy was about to go upstairs, when she heard someone calling her name. To her surprise, there was Erin, getting out of a car.

"Isn't that your friend Erin?" Dr. Wallace asked. "You weren't expecting her, were you?"

Kathy shook her head. By then Erin was upon them, and it was clear from the look on her face that there was something very wrong.

"Shall I leave you girls alone?" Dr. Wallace asked, directing the question more to Erin than to Kathy.

"Please," Erin said, in a voice that was barely audible.

As soon as her father was out of earshot, Kathy asked, "What's wrong? You look awful."

"I have to give you something." Stiffly, Erin reached into the pocket of her jeans, brought out the pearl bracelet, and shoved it into Kathy's hand.

"What's this . . . oh, my bracelet." Kathy looked at

Erin in confusion. "Was it in one of those pairs of shorts I gave you?"

"No."

"So you found it at my house?" Kathy asked, still trying to get the story straight. "Thanks for returning it. I'm really awful with jewelry. I bet it was under the bed or—"

"I didn't find it, Kathy," Erin interrupted. "I took it."

# Six

"Took it?" Kathy couldn't believe she was hearing Erin correctly.

"To keep."

*She stole it.* The words reverberated in Kathy's head, but they still didn't make much sense.

"I'm sorry, Kathy," Erin said, a mixture of shame and defiance dripping from every syllable.

"Let's go sit in the lobby," Kathy said. "I want to know what's going on."

"My mom's waiting for me," Erin said, indicating the car. She didn't want to have a heart-to-heart talk with Kathy. She just wanted to go home and forget this whole miserable episode.

But Kathy wasn't about to let it alone. Erin could be

brash, belligerent even, but a thief? That wasn't the Erin that she knew. "No way, Erin," Kathy insisted. "I'm not letting you go until I've heard the whole story."

"All right, all right," Erin ran over to the car, and Kathy saw Mrs. Moriarity nod her head. When she came back, Erin said without preamble, "Your bracelet dropped on the floor while I was trying on things, and I took it."

"But why?"

*Why?* Erin wondered. How could she answer Kathy when she wasn't sure herself. "Because I was mad at you, I guess," Erin finally said.

"Mad?" Kathy asked, more confused than ever. "But we weren't having a fight or anything."

Tears welled up in Erin's eyes. "I was mad because you had so much stuff, and I couldn't even go back to camp!" There, she had said it.

"You're not going back to Wildwood?" Kathy said in a shocked voice.

"There wasn't a scholarship this year, and my folks don't have enough money to send me."

Kathy felt terrible. "Why didn't you tell us?"

"What good would that have done?" Erin asked bitterly. "You couldn't do anything about it."

"But you just sat there at the picnic while we were making all those plans. You must have known then. And today, when Jill and I were saying we might not get back to camp. You could have told us this afternoon."

"It wasn't the same. I didn't have some other place to go this summer, like you two did." More quietly, she added, "It was too humiliating to tell you I didn't have the money to go."

Kathy didn't know what to say.

"Look, you can let the others know I'm not going to camp, but don't tell them about the bracelet, okay?" There was a pleading note in Erin's voice.

"No, no. I won't say anything. But Erin . . ."

"I've got to go." Erin turned away. Then she looked back and said, "I'm really sorry, Kathy."

"I know," Kathy whispered softly. She watched as Erin, her shoulders slumped, walked back to the car.

Erin didn't know when she had felt more awful. She was so ashamed. As she climbed into the car, Mrs. Moriarity said, "Are you all right, Erin?"

Erin nodded. "Kathy was nice about it. She was almost as embarrassed as I was."

"At least you made it right."

Erin thought back over the events of the day. She

certainly hadn't expected to wind up at Kathy's house
this evening. Even though she had been uncomfortable chatting to her dad with Kathy's bracelet in her
pocket, she'd had no intention of giving it back. It was
as if the bracelet were going to make up for all the
angry and hurt feelings she had about missing camp.

When she had come home, her mother was out in
their tiny backyard, gardening. Mrs. Moriarity ad-
justed her sun hat and looked up at Erin. "Do you
want to help me?"

Erin shrugged. "Are you planting?"

"Weeding."

"Weeding is so boring," Erin said grumpily, but nev-
ertheless, she got down on her knees and began
pulling up a few weeds.

"Well, you know, honey, weeding is a lot like life."

"How's that?" Erin said, though she wasn't particularly interested in finding out.

"Your life is like your garden, with all sorts of pretty
flowers, and yes, some practical vegetables in it. Then
the weeds start coming up and choking off some of the
plants. Some of the weeds are not so easily recogniz-
able, some may even be nice looking. But they're still
weeds. If you're watchful and take care of them early
on, they don't cause any problems. But if you let the

weeding slide, pretty soon there's no wonderful garden anymore."

Erin thought about this for a moment, then she said, "Mom, that is the corniest thing you've ever said."

Her mother burst into laughter. "Yeah, it is, but that doesn't mean it's not true."

Erin tried to put her mother's little lecture aside. It was so silly. Besides, so what if your garden was full of weeds? Weeds were tough. She reached across the fuzzy little carrot plants and forced a leafy weed out of the ground. Wasn't it better to be strong like that? If you were strong, it wouldn't be so easy to get hurt.

Standing up, Erin said, "I guess weeding's too hard for me, Mom. It hurts my knees."

Mrs. Moriarity stood up, too. "I'm done, too, for a while." She put her arm around Erin as they walked inside. It made Erin feel uncomfortable, and she shrugged it off.

"What's wrong?" her mother asked.

"Nothing."

Mrs. Moriarity stopped Erin in her tracks and lifted her face toward her. "Erin, I know all my children, and I know when something's not right with them. Tell me."

Erin had just shaken her head and hurried up to her room. Reaching into her pocket, and pulling the bracelet out, seeing it there, really there in her bedroom, made her feel slightly sick to her stomach. What was she going to do with it? Shoving it into a drawer, Erin hoped that maybe if she put the bracelet out of sight she could forget about it. But even in the drawer, its presence pervaded the room.

*I'll probably never get another good night's sleep in here,* Erin thought. She lay down on her bed and cried for a little while. Then she went downstairs, took a deep breath, and told her mother the truth.

Erin hadn't been very surprised by her mother's reaction. Her expression was hurt and dismayed. But as often happened when her children really messed up, she didn't get angry. She tried, instead, to figure out what went wrong, and how to make the situation better.

Despite intense questioning, Erin would only say she had taken the bracelet and she didn't know why. Then, at her mother's urging, she had gone over to Kathy's.

But now that they were alone in the car together heading back home, Erin knew that the questions were going to start again. This time, she felt more ready to answer them. But first she said, "You don't have to tell Daddy, do you?"

"Erin, you know I don't keep secrets from your father."

"But it's all finished now."

Mrs. Moriarity sighed "It's not finished. We haven't even started on this, not really. And we won't until you tell me what was in your head when you pocketed that bracelet."

"I was mad," Erin said, some of her rebelliousness sneaking back into her voice.

"About camp, I suppose?"

"About . . . everything."

"I thought you learned some lessons about money at Christmas," Mrs. Moriarity said.

"I know that. . . . It's just that the girls were always planning the summer, and everything we were going to do at camp, and I could never find the right minute to tell them I wasn't going. . . ." Erin's voice trailed off.

"And you felt like you might even the score with the world if you took Kathy's bracelet."

When her mother said it like that, it sounded pretty stupid. "I guess."

Mrs. Moriarity just shook her head sadly.

The car finally chug-chugged its way home. Erin

wished that there were one thing that worked the way it was supposed to around her house.

She was hoping her father wouldn't be home for a while, and he wasn't. Erin was dreading this particular confrontation, but when Mr. Moriarity burst through the door, there was no mistaking his wonderful mood.

"Joe, what's happened?" Mrs. Moriarity asked.

Instead of answering, he picked her up and whirled her around the room. Danny and Jeanette looked at them in amazement.

"Put me down," she laughed. "And tell me what's going on with you."

Mr. Moriarity reached into his pocket, pulled something out, and began waving it around.

Maureen jumped out of her chair. "It's a lottery ticket! Did you win? Did you win?"

"Maybe," he teased.

"You mean we're millionaires?" The color drained from Mrs. Moriarity's face.

"Oh no, no." Mr. Moriarity calmed down a little. "We didn't win the big prize. I only got three out of five numbers. But that was worth over three thousand dollars."

"It sounds like a fortune to me," Mrs. Moriarity

said, recovering her composure and giving her husband a hug.

The family spent the rest of the evening sitting around talking about all the things they might do with this sudden windfall. Erin, still feeling guilty about the day's events, didn't participate too much. Despite her awareness of how many things they needed, and what needed to be repaired, hearing them all listed, one after another, was a little disconcerting. Besides the car, the dryer needed to be fixed, and the washer wasn't in great shape either. Maureen suggested that they have the house painted, and her mother wished they could have the lawn resodded. Pat and Mike wanted to go on a vacation, and to Erin's surprise, her parents didn't say no.

"It's been a long time since we've all gotten away together," Mrs. Moriarity said with a faraway look on her face. "Remember that cabin we used to rent in Michigan when Maureen was a baby?"

"I don't remember," Maureen said indignantly. "Even when I'm around, I miss out on the good stuff."

Mr. Moriarity laughed. "You couldn't have been more than a year old. Catching fish during the day, grilling them at night. The nights were as black as velvet. You could see every little star," he reminisced.

"Maybe there will be a little money left over for a vacation," his wife said softly.

*At least that would be some consolation for missing camp,* Erin thought.

By the time she went to bed, some of the excitement had calmed down. Still, Erin didn't think her mother would bring her dad down off his lottery high by telling him about the stolen bracelet. But when Erin got up early the next morning, she heard her parents talking in the kitchen.

They must have realized she was up and walking around, because when she was done in the bathroom, Erin saw her mother standing at the top of the stairs.

"Can you come down?"

Erin nodded. She went into her bedroom, got her robe, and went downstairs thinking, *Uh-oh.*

Jeanette was the only one of the other children who was up, and even though she was too young to understand what was going on, she still seemed to sense that something was. As she played on the floor, she looked curiously at her parents, who were solemnly drinking their coffee.

"Good morning," Erin said, wondering if there was any chance of that being true.

Her mother didn't waste any time. "I told your father what happened yesterday."

Erin could feel her eyes filling with tears. "I'm sorry, Daddy."

"No, I'm sorry," he murmured. "I feel really bad about camp."

"It's okay."

"I've been talking to your mother, Erin," Mr. Moriarity said, taking a sip of his coffee. "I think maybe we should use the lottery money for at least a partial session at that camp of yours."

Erin was stunned. "But Dad," she stammered, "I should be punished for what I did. Not rewarded."

Mr. Moriarity's laugh was short. "That's probably true. But it hurts me to think you were so angry that you'd resort to thievery. Erin, I know you're a good child. If you took this bracelet, you must have been beside yourself with all kinds of ugly feelings."

Erin ran into her father's arms and started to cry. He knew how she felt, exactly how she felt. And incredibly, he didn't seem to be mad at her.

Mr. Moriarity pulled her away from him and looked into her eyes "So what do you say, little girl? Should we use that money for camp?"

A part of Erin wanted to say, "Yes! I can't wait!" But

there was another part, too; the part that remembered hearing the list of things the family needed, things that would make all their lives more pleasant, not just the life of one of its members. She thought about how much everyone wanted to go on vacation. Was it fair that she would be the only one spending time in the country this summer?

"No, we shouldn't," Erin whispered.

"You don't think so?" her father asked again.

"It wouldn't be right." No, she thought, using that money for camp would be as wrong as stealing the bracelet.

Now Mr. Moriarity's hug was even tighter. "I would have sent you, hon. I wanted you to make the choice. I think it's the right one."

# SEVEN

Jill dreamed a fly was buzzing around her head as she spun on the ice rink. She kept trying to swat the bug away, but just as she was about to go into a fabulous spin, back it came. Then the fly was buzzing around her toes. She looked down at her feet. She wasn't wearing any skates! She was so shocked, she woke up, and saw Owen standing at the foot of her bed, laughing at her.

"Mom told me to wake you up," he said.

"I'm sure she didn't tell you to tickle me up," Jill responded grumpily.

"She didn't say not to."

"Oh go away. Git!"

Still grinning, Owen left Jill in bed, where she

closed her eyes once more. She didn't want to get up. The day she had ahead of her was way too full. First church, then skating practice, then going to a competition where one of her friends was skating, and finally, homework, with that science project still to finish up and a composition to write. Jill groaned. All she wanted to do was snuggle under the covers and stay there. But knowing everyone was waiting motivated her to get up and get dressed.

"We're going to be late for church," her mother fussed when she got downstairs. "And your breakfast is getting cold."

Jill saw the waffles on her plate but they looked naked without syrup and butter. "Please pass the syrup," Jill tried.

"Now, you know Tony said you have to watch your weight," said Mrs. Lewis.

"He didn't say I was fat," Jill said indignantly.

"You don't want to look like a whale on skates, do you?" Owen asked.

Jill gave him a withering glance. "I want syrup!"

"All right, I don't have time to argue." Her mother poured some syrup onto her plate. Jill ate the waffles, but she couldn't say she enjoyed them. She was well aware that Tony had suggested she keep her weight stabilized by sticking to a low-fat diet. That meant leaving out a lot of foods that she liked. After breakfast, she had to run around getting her skating gear so she could be dropped off at the rink right after church.

Jill didn't really start to calm down until she got to church. There was something about walking into the sanctuary that brought a blanket of peace to her, no matter what else was going on in her life.

She liked everything about the Mt. Zion Baptist Church. She liked the way everyone greeted her as though she was part of a family, and she liked the way the church looked, with its small stained-glass windows and its rough, worn pews. But most of all she liked the singing. There was nothing like the energetic cadence of gospel music to make you feel as though things were right with the world—or if they weren't now, they soon would be.

Jill's mother was in the choir, and although Jill knew that hours of rehearsal went into the music, the members always looked as if there was no place they would rather be than singing, swaying, and praising with their songs. Jill had always thought that one day she might like to be a part of the choir. She had inherited her mom's lovely soprano voice, and high school kids could join. But sitting there listening to *Take My Hand, Precious Lord,* Jill knew that singing in the choir would take up way too much of her time. She wondered how many other things she might miss out on if she decided to devote the next six years or so to skating.

Later at the rink, as Jill skated out to find Tony, she looked longingly outside through the big plate-glass window. It was a gorgeous day, sunny and just the right kind of warm, and all the flowers were bursting into bloom. Her family was spending the day at the botanic garden, a perfect choice for an afternoon outing. Reluctantly, Jill turned away from the window and skated over to Tony, who was helping another student with his turns.

"Oh hi, Jill," he said absently. "Start practicing those axels until I'm ready for you."

*Axels,* Jill thought and sighed, but dutifully she began practicing them. Ever since this camp thing had come up, skating hadn't seemed as much fun as it used to. Taking her parents' request to heart, Jill had been trying to figure out where skating fit into her life. She felt the pressure of knowing that not only this summer but maybe the rest of her life hinged on this one decision. All the peace she had found in church that morning disappeared like smoke into the air. Her burden must have showed in her skating, because when Tony finally got over to her, he said, "You're skating as if you've got lead weights attached to your legs."

Jill stopped. "Am I?"

"You know that skating is a combination of grace and skill. Frankly, at the moment, you're showing neither."

Normally, Jill could take this sort of criticism, and sometimes it even spurred her to work harder. But not today. Today, Jill could feel the tears coming to her eyes. This was such an unusual response that Tony looked concerned for a moment. "Are you okay?" he asked.

Jill gulped. "I've just got a lot on my mind."

Tony nodded. "It's about skating camp, isn't it? Your mother called me yesterday and asked if I could talk to you."

"I'm not sure what I should do."

Tony said, "Let's sit down for a few minutes, Jill."

Gratefully, Jill skated over to the bench, and Tony followed behind her.

"You know, this shouldn't be such a hard decision for you to make."

"It shouldn't?" Jill asked with surprise.

"No." Tony's hand swept out toward the rink. "Most of these kids, especially the good ones, would love a chance to go to skating camp."

Jill began to feel guilty. "Well, I think it's a good opportunity too," she said defensively. "I just had my heart set on going back to Camp Wildwood."

Tony looked at her a bit oddly. "You mean you feel as strongly about going back to that camp of yours as you do about skating?"

"No, it's not the same," Jill replied, feeling as though Tony was trying to trip her up with a trick question. "I know that skating is more important than spending the summer with my friends."

"I hear a 'but' at the end of that sentence," Tony said, waiting to hear the rest.

"But I want to have fun, too." She blurted it out before she even had a chance to hear the words in her head.

"Jill, you've read books about skaters and other athletes. I'm sure there were times that they wanted to have fun, too, but they had a goal and they worked toward it and didn't let anything else get in the way." Tony looked at her sternly. "Can you say the same thing?"

"But those skaters, the ones I read about in books, they made it to the top."

"Look," Tony said, a little more gently, "you have a lot of talent. How much? That really won't be evident for a while. But you know you started late, Jill, and a topflight skating career takes more than time. It takes money. I won't kid you. You could work your tail off and still not make it in the world of serious competition. The odds are against you."

Tony wasn't painting a very pretty picture of her future, Jill thought. But she knew he was trying to be honest. She wondered how she would feel if she did nothing but skate for the next couple of years and then still didn't make the grade.

"The only thing to do," Tom continued, "is keep at it. Taking the summer off," he added bluntly, "would be a step backward. But maybe you don't want to make skating your life. Heaven knows I wouldn't tell anyone to put up with this crazy regime if she wasn't dedicated to it. Now, let's get back to practice."

Jill put extra effort into her skating, and by the end of the session, Tony seemed pleased. "You look much better than you did at the start of the session." It was a backhanded compliment, but a compliment nonetheless. Jill was glad that Tony had softened toward her, because he was going to be driving her and Lily Chu to Lily's competition this afternoon. The last thing she wanted to do was spend half an hour in the car with a grumpy coach.

Lily was a little younger than Jill, but very good, and a friendly rivalry had developed between the girls. Jill had been just over the age limit for this competition, which she had won last year, but Lily was able to participate, and she had asked Jill a long time ago if she would come and watch her. Despite all the mixed feelings Jill was having about skating, she still wanted to go and support her friend.

Lily had been off in another corner of the rink practicing her routine diligently. When they finally piled into the car, Lily seemed excited but confident.

"I saw your practicing," Jill said, turning around to look at Lily in the backseat. "You looked great."

"I've been at the rink every day for months. Some days twice. I'm glad it shows."

When Tony stopped to get gas and was safely out of earshot, Jill said, a little hesitantly, "Lily, does all the practice ever get to you?"

"What do you mean?" Lily asked, puzzled.

"I mean, don't you ever get tired of having to fit everything in your life around skating?"

Lily shook her head. "No. Skating is my life."

As they continued their ride, Jill closed her eyes and pretended to be sleeping, but actually she was thinking, maybe harder than she ever had. When Lily said it, she was so sure. Skating was her life and everything else came second. Jill knew in her heart of hearts that she didn't feel that way about skating at all. She loved flying around the rink, and winning prizes was wonderful. Perhaps best of all were her daydreams about becoming the Queen of the Ice. Yet in the real world there were many other things that made her happy. She liked to read and sing; sometimes she even fantasized about being a singer. If she had put as much time into singing lessons as into skating, would she now be considering that her career?

Watching Lily at the competition only heightened the feelings Jill had been having on the way over to the rink. Jill rarely had the luxury of being at a skating event as a nonparticipant. Usually, she tried not to watch her fellow competitors because she didn't want to make herself nervous. So it was her habit to wait off the rink, barely paying attention to what was happening on the ice.

Now, sitting in the stands, Jill watched, really watched, as the skaters came out to go through their paces. Clearly, she was better than many of the kids, especially the younger ones. However, Lily and several others were excellent. They had a fluidity of form and an exuberance of spirit that Jill was not at all sure she could match. Seeing Lily twirling into a spin, Jill realized that Lily and these others were her competition. It was going to take years and more years of sweat and tears to be able to match and eventually surpass them.

And suddenly, it was quite clear to Jill that this was *not* how she wanted to spend the next decade or so. It wasn't because of all the effort involved either. Jill knew that if becoming a top-notch skater were her ambition, nothing it took to make it become a reality would be too hard.

But for her, skating was more a lovely fantasy, not a burning desire. It wasn't everything. Not the way it probably was for Lily and certainly for the greats of the skating world. Jill loved skating, but she didn't love it so much she was willing to trade all the other areas of her life for it.

"I just don't want to," she whispered to herself, and then a peculiar sensation came over Jill. She felt much lighter and airier. To her great amazement, she also felt as if she'd like nothing so much as to take a spin around the rink. She imagined that would feel as it had when she first started skating. As if she was doing it just for fun.

# EIGHT

Kathy looked idly around downtown Evanston as she waited for Jill and Lia to appear in front of the Gap. Kathy was finished with school for the year, but Jill and Lia still had another week to go. That's why she had arrived early for their pre-camp shopping trip.

Catching sight of herself in the store's big picture window, Kathy was slightly surprised to see how tall she had grown. With her hair pulled back, and wearing the new silver earrings her grandmother had sent her, Kathy felt she looked like a high school kid instead of someone just finishing seventh grade. It made her feel a little odd, and she turned away from her reflection. She practically bumped into Lia.

"Jill called last night and said she was going to be

late, so we should just get started," Lia said without preamble.

"Is she at skating practice?" Kathy asked.

Lia shook her head. "Since she decided not to go to skating camp, she's cut back on her practice here, too."

"Wow," Kathy said. "She's really done an about-face."

"She's not going to drop skating. She's just taking the summer off. No pressure for a while."

Kathy wished she could say the same about her own life. All the plans for Europe had been changed and revised to a week in London at the end of the summer. Despite giving in, Dr. Wallace still seemed upset about the whole thing, and not so much with Anne, but with her. Sometimes Kathy thought that she had the worst of both worlds with her dad. She didn't get to see him all that much, and when she did, they were often butting heads.

Not wanting to think about family matters, Kathy turned her attention to shopping with a vengeance. By the time Jill joined them, Kathy had already picked out two pairs of shorts, three tees, a baseball cap, and a sweatshirt for the chillier nights. When she looked down at the pile of clothes in her arms as she was checking out, Kathy did feel a little guilty. No wonder Erin felt jealous of Kathy's material wealth. On the other hand, Erin was rich when it came to family. Maybe having a great family didn't seem so important when you were going to be looking at them all summer.

Kathy sighed. Here she was right back where she didn't want to be, thinking about families.

"What's wrong?" Lia asked as she joined her at the checkout counter. She was buying a pair of jeans.

Before Kathy could answer, Jill came up with her own purchases. "Are we done shopping?"

"I am," Kathy said a bit ruefully.

"I still want to look at bathing suits," Lia replied.

"There's a store a couple of blocks down that has some really cute suits in the window," Jill informed her. "Let's hit that one as soon as we're done here."

Kathy was thankful that at least she didn't need a new bathing suit. Even just watching the agony that Lia and Jill were going through as they tried on suit after suit in the crowded dressing room wasn't much fun.

"I think this one makes me look stubby," Jill said, trying to look over her shoulder in the mirror. "I'm right, aren't I?"

"No, you look fine," Lia replied, too caught up in her own suit dilemma to really give Jill much of a glance. "But what about this one? Do you think I'd look better in a two-piece?"

Kathy was beginning to lose patience. "You both look fine. Why don't you just get the suits you're wearing, and we can go?"

Lia and Jill turned to Kathy in amazement. "This is only the fourth suit I've tried on," Jill said.

Lia added, "Boys are going to be seeing us in these suits all summer."

"Oh, boys," Kathy said disdainfully. If there was one thing that bugged her about her Holiday Five friends, it was that in her opinion they thought way too much about boys. First it had been Lia and her next-door neighbor, Scott, then it was Maddy and a boy she liked named Tony, and of course, one of the things about camp that Erin was going to miss most was Cal. Only Jill had seemed as aloof from boys as Kathy did, and Kathy guessed that was because she was so involved with her skating. Now that Jill had more time, she'd probably be just as much interested in the opposite sex.

It wasn't that Kathy disliked boys. There were several guys in her class that she was friends with. Last summer in Wildwood, Marty Robertson had developed a real thing for Kathy, and she'd mildly encouraged it. But as for really liking a boy, the way Lia liked Scott, for instance, that hadn't happened yet, and Kathy wasn't expecting it to. She would be perfectly content to watch the Fourth of July fireworks at camp all by herself.

"Kathy, wait until you find a boy you like," Lia said. "Then you'll wish you had spent more time picking out bathing suits."

"That's going to be a long wait," Kathy said witheringly. "Now, how many more suits do you guys want to try on?"

There were quite a few, and then both Lia and Jill left without buying anything, preferring to keep looking for that perfect bathing suit that they knew was out there somewhere.

Dr. Wallace, who was having a consultation with another doctor at Evanston Hospital, had arranged to pick up Kathy at Jill's house. After Lia said good-bye, Kathy and Jill went back there.

No one was home. They went up to Jill's room, and Kathy immediately began circling the room, looking at Jill's skating memorabilia.

"So are you going to miss it?" Kathy asked curiously.

"I'd be lying if I said I won't." Jill came up behind Kathy, who was looking at her trophy. "I guess I thought all my problems would be solved once I made a decision about skating, but it seems like I have to keep deciding stuff over and over again."

"Such as?" Kathy wanted to know.

"Oh, how much time I should put in on skating. And if I should keep seeing my old friends from the rink."

"Why shouldn't you?"

Jill shrugged. "It feels weird. I saw one of the girls, Lily, the other day, and she just couldn't understand how I could give up on serious skating. It was like all of a sudden we had nothing in common."

"What about your parents?" Kathy wanted to know. "How are they taking it?"

"I think they're relieved," Jill said quietly. "I mean, they've always said they would support me whatever I wanted to do, but big-time skating would mean finding sponsors and getting endorsements, maybe even moving to another city with better facilities."

Kathy was shocked. She had thought all there was to skating was getting out on the ice.

"The hardest thing," Jill said softly, "was admitting to myself I probably wasn't good enough or determined enough to get that far."

"You know what I think you are?"

Jill shook her head.

"Smart. Smart enough to figure out what you really wanted."

A smile appeared on Jill's face. "I appreciate that. I do."

"Now, me, I don't want to think about anything or figure anything out for the next couple of months. I just want to enjoy camp."

"We will," Jill said. Then she added, "Too bad we won't be enjoying it with Erin."

Kathy had told the others about Erin not going back to camp, though she had kept her word about keeping the story of the bracelet to herself. Naturally, when the other girls heard the news, they had all called Erin, but each had gotten the same response, a few curt answers and a lot of silence at the other end of the phone.

"Isn't there anything we can do?" Jill asked Kathy plaintively.

"If there is, I don't know what," Kathy answered. "Without a scholarship, Erin just doesn't have enough money to go back. Even if we could come up with the money, she'd be too embarrassed to take it."

Despite her certainty that there was nothing that

could be done for Erin, when Kathy was having dinner out with her dad later that evening, the topic came up again. She explained the situation and said to Dr. Wallace, "Am I missing something? Is there any way to get Erin back to camp?"

Dr. Wallace swallowed a bite of his linguine. "I don't think so. Unless there were some other scholarship available for Erin, and frankly it's much too late in the game to start looking around for those."

"Another scholarship," Kathy said thoughtfully.

"You know of one?" Dr. Wallace asked with surprise.

"Not exactly, Dad. But you've given me an idea. A definite idea."

"I don't get it," Erin said to her mother, who was standing in her bedroom doorway. "School has been out for exactly one day. I should at least get to sleep in for one day. And here it is, nine o'clock in the morning, and I'm getting dressed to go somewhere on some mystery errand." She shook her head.

"I think this is one excursion you won't mind getting up early for," Mrs. Moriarity said with a smile. "Come down and have your breakfast as soon as you're ready."

Erin turned back to her closet. She didn't even know what she was supposed to wear. This had all come up yesterday after her mother had gotten a phone call. Erin hadn't paid much attention. She had been playing a game of checkers with Danny, and although she heard her name mentioned, Erin figured it was the doctor or dentist confirming an appointment.

Erin hadn't thought any more about it until much later that evening. The younger kids were in bed, and Maureen was out with her friends. Her parents called her into the kitchen, and her mom said, "Remember that phone call I had earlier in the evening?"

"Yes," Erin said warily.

"Well, it's about a surprise."

"For me?" Erin was surprised already. "Tell me, Mom."

"That's just it. I promised, well, the people responsible, that I would just bring you to the appointed place at the appointed time, and you'd find out then."

Erin turned to her father. "Dad?"

Her father's grin was wide. "Nope. You'll just have to wait it out. But it's a nice surprise, I can tell you that."

Erin teased a little bit more for details, but she couldn't get much out of her parents, only that the event would take place in Chicago, and that she wouldn't be the only person there.

Finally deciding to wear a new pair of shorts and a fresh T-shirt, Erin also put on a pair of small hoop earrings and went down to breakfast. She had slept surprisingly soundly, but the moment she woke up her first thought was of her mysterious expedition. She wondered if it had something to do with the family's lottery win, but she didn't think it could, since most of the money had already been spent on necessities. A small amount had been put aside for a vacation at the Wisconsin Dells, but they wouldn't be going until the end of the summer, so Erin didn't see how today's event could be connected to that.

Whatever was going on, Erin hoped it was something that was going to perk up her summer. She had waited too long to answer Gina about their babysitting venture. Gina had asked another girl to be her partner. Now Erin was going to have to find other sitting jobs or spend most of her days taking care of her own siblings.

"What time are we supposed to be . . . wherever we're supposed to be?" Erin asked as she gobbled her cereal.

"In about a half hour," her mother replied. "Your

dad said to tell you he hopes this makes you as happy as he thinks it will."

"Who's going to stay with the kids?"

"I am," said Maureen coming into the room. "Did anyone ever tell you you were one lucky kid?"

Erin looked at Maureen carefully. Her sister seemed torn between graciousness and jealousy. "Yeah, I guess I am," Erin said softly.

A half hour later, Erin was in the car with her mother, heading up Lake Shore Drive. When Mrs. Moriarity turned off the drive and began down a small street with inviting-looking homes, something in Erin's mind clicked. "Hey, I've been here before."

"But at night," Mrs. Moriarity said. She pulled into the driveway. "Remember this house?"

Erin nodded, surprised. "It belongs to Mrs. Tillman. The owner of Camp Wildwood."

# NINE

"This has something to do with camp?" Erin asked wonderingly as she and her mom climbed the steps to the camp director's home.

"You're getting warm," Mrs. Moriarity said, smiling. Then she knocked at the door.

Mrs. Tillman greeted Erin and her mother and drew them inside. The last time Erin had been in the house was at a winter reunion Mrs. Tillman had thrown for her campers. Then the house had been decorated with snowmen and candy canes and Santas everywhere. Now it looked more like a ghost house ready for Halloween, with sheets draping the chairs and other furniture.

"You must forgive the way the house looks, but I'm

leaving this afternoon for Wildwood, and I close this place down for the summer." She led the Moriaritys toward her office. "Have you told her anything?" she asked Erin's mother.

"Not enough to give the surprise away."

Mrs. Tillman opened the door to her office, and the first thing Erin saw was Lia and Kathy with big smiles on their faces.

"What are you guys doing here?" she asked, as she felt hope rising inside her.

Mrs. Tillman turned to Kathy. "Why don't you tell her, since this was your idea?"

"You're going to camp!" Kathy squealed.

"I am?"

"Yes, you are," Mrs. Tillman confirmed. "If you don't mind a little work to make it happen."

"I don't mind," Erin answered quickly, "but I still don't understand . . ."

"Kathy called me yesterday and told me all about your situation and how much you wanted to come back to Wildwood. Since Family Services didn't have any money this year, she suggested that perhaps the camp could offer a scholarship to you. We've never done that before, but Kathy made an eloquent case for there being a first time. I have to admit, I didn't immediately think it was a good idea. But finally Kathy and I compromised: a scholarship to camp, and in return you will help out in the dining hall for five meals a week."

Erin could feel the tears welling up in her eyes. She usually hated crying in public, but today it didn't seem to matter. "I . . . I don't know what to say, Mrs. Tillman, except thank you." She turned to Kathy. "How did you come up with the idea?"

Kathy smiled. "What is that my dad always tells me? Necessity is the mother of invention? It was absolutely necessary that you come back to Wildwood, so I had to figure out something. My dad and I were talking about scholarships, and it just hit me."

"Thank you," Erin said softly. There was much more she wanted to say to Kathy. After pocketing Kathy's bracelet, Erin had thought she'd ruined their friendship. Instead, Kathy had still been trying to think of ways to get her to camp. That meant as much to Erin as actually being able to spend the summer with her friends.

"Jill and Maddy wanted to be here, but they couldn't make it," Lia said, "so we're the representatives for Bunk Three." Lia turned to Mrs. Tillman. "We are going to be able to bunk together, aren't we?"

"After all the trouble you girls went to to be together? I'm not going to keep you apart now. By the way," Mrs. Tillman continued, "since Kathy came to me with her idea, I've been thinking quite a bit about scholarships. As I said, at first I didn't think they were a very good idea."

"Why not?" Lia asked.

"It would mean decisions about who would get them, and applications, and to be rather blunt, less room for the paying customers. But after reflecting on it, I decided those were all selfish reasons not to offer scholarships. Still, I think young people value something more if they have to work for it. So each year I'm going to give out two working scholarships, to a girl and a boy camper."

"I'm glad," Mrs. Moriarity said.

"And Kathy," Mrs. Tillman said, "I'll make sure that whenever we award a scholarship, I'll tell them your story and how you went out on a limb for a friend."

Kathy's expression was equal parts pleasure and embarrassment.

"Your name's going down in Camp Wildwood history," Lia said teasingly. "The campers will never forget you."

"I never will," Erin murmured. "That's for sure."

———

"Now are you sure you have everything, Kathy?" Dr. Wallace fretted. He was standing in the middle of her bedroom in the house at Lake Pointe, looking around with frustration. Kathy's mother had needed to go out of town on an emergency business trip, so Dr. Wallace had been assigned the task of getting Kathy off to camp.

"Mom sent the trunk before she left. All I had to do was pack a bag of things I needed right away."

"Then what's all this?" her father asked, gesturing to the piles of clothes, books, magazines, and jewelry that dotted the room.

"This is the stuff that isn't going."

"Well, it's not going to stay here all summer, is it?"

Kathy had sort of hoped that Mrs. Curtis might put the rejects away after she left, but with her father standing so sternly in the middle of the mess, she decided perhaps she'd best make an effort to clean up.

As Kathy began shoving clothes back into drawers, Dr. Wallace said, "Your mother told me something before she left."

Kathy tried to think if she had done anything particularly horrible lately. Nothing came to mind.

"She told me about that event at Mrs. Tillman's house."

"Oh that." Kathy had told her father about suggesting the scholarship to a receptive Mrs. Tillman, but she hadn't filled him in on Erin's surprise.

"Yes, that. You know you did a very wonderful thing, Kathy."

Kathy piled some books on her bookshelf, her face turned away from her father. "Yeah, whatever."

Gently, Dr. Wallace pulled her toward him. "Not whatever. You should be very proud of yourself. You made something happen for a friend."

Kathy thought back to her meeting with Mrs. Tillman. As the camp owner had told Erin, she hadn't been a pushover about it. When Kathy had explained about Erin's situation, Mrs. Tillman had sympathized, but after the conversation had gone back and forth, she finally told Kathy she didn't see what could be done, that the camp was in business to make money.

"You may not realize it, Kathy, but we have lots of expenses at camp—food, upkeep, insurance. I can't just go around letting campers in for free."

That had made Kathy mad.

"All our parents pay a lot for us to go to camp. And

some kids don't even appreciate it. It seems like there should be something left over for kids who really want to come and can't afford it."

Mrs. Tillman had been shocked at Kathy's boldness. For a minute, Kathy thought the woman was going to order her out of the house or perhaps even tell her she couldn't return to camp. But then Mrs. Tillman's weathered face had cracked a smile. "I don't see how I can argue with that."

"You can't?"

"No. Let me think about this, and I'll get back to you. Camp Wildwood should be in the business of giving something back to the community, too."

That evening, she had called Kathy and told her that some work had to be part of the scholarship. If Erin agreed, she would be Wildwood's first scholarship recipient.

Dr. Wallace put his hand under his daughter's chin and looked into her eyes. "When you first said you'd rather go to camp than to Europe, I thought you were just being contrary. I didn't understand what camp meant to you. I do now. And I'm very proud of you. I guess I don't tell you that often enough."

Kathy wasn't sure he had ever told her, but hearing it now made her feel wonderful.

Giving his daughter a quick hug, Dr. Wallace said, "Now, let's get this room in shape so we can get going. After all this, I'd hate for you to miss the bus."

The bus station was a madhouse when they arrived. Apparently there were more camps than just Wildwood loading up. At first Kathy couldn't find her friends. Then she saw Jill waving to her from beside a bus over in the corner.

"There they are," she told her father.

"Shall I say good-bye now?"

Kathy gave her father a big hug. "I'll write."

"You'd better," said Dr. Wallace, kissing the top of her head. "I'll miss you."

Then Kathy ran over to join her friends.

"I thought you weren't going to make it," Lia scolded. "We're just about to board."

"I hope we get to sit together," Maddy said, noting how many kids were crowding around the front of the bus.

Erin pulled Kathy aside. "I know I called you and thanked you, Kathy, but—"

Kathy interrupted her. "Hey, I didn't get you to camp so you'd spend the whole summer thanking me."

"All the things you did, and didn't do, like telling about the bracelet. They mean a lot to me. That's it.

Not another word until you do something else nice for me," Erin said with a grin.

Kathy laughed and followed the surging group of kids onto the bus. The girls naturally assumed that they would sit together, even though with five, one of them would have to sit separately. But with all the kids fighting for a seat, Kathy got separated from her friends and was pushed to the back, even as the other girls found four seats together at the front of the bus.

When Lia looked over her shoulder and caught Kathy's eye, Kathy just shrugged and took a seat. She had a book in her bag, and depending on who her seatmate was, she would just read all the way to Wisconsin. Almost immediately, someone slid into the seat next to her.

It was a boy about her age, but what a boy. His dark straight hair was on the longish side and fell around a face that resembled one of Kathy's favorite TV stars. It was easy to see that he was taller than she was, which was not often the case with boys Kathy's age. All in all, he looked just about perfect, except for one thing—the sullen expression on his face.

Kathy was sure that he was new at Wildwood. If he had been around last summer, the girls would have noticed. Despite the vibes he was giving off, Kathy decided that she might at least make an effort to be friendly.

As the bus started noisily out of the shelter, Kathy turned to the boy and said, "Hi."

The boy seemed surprised that she was willing to penetrate the wall he so clearly wanted up around him. After a beat or two, he gruffly said, "Hi."

"So I guess you don't want to be going to Wildwood."

"Camp." He practically spat out the word. "A place where your parents can park you while they're off doing their own thing."

"What are they doing?" Kathy asked.

"Going to Europe. They get Paris, I get Wisconsin," he said bitterly.

Kathy didn't feel this was the time to say she had passed up a trip to Europe so she could come to camp.

The boy turned to her. "Don't you think we're a little old to be going to camp?"

Kathy shrugged. "It's not like we're off playing with the eight-year-olds. Horseback riding, swimming, that's stuff anybody can enjoy."

"Well, not me," the boy said with determination.

Kathy found herself getting a little irritated. It was one thing not to want to go to camp, but it was another to ruin the whole summer just because things hadn't gone your way. Kathy reached into her bag and pulled out her book. No matter how cute he was, they were clearly bugging each other.

While Kathy read, the boy closed his eyes, though she didn't think he was really sleeping. After a while, with his eyes still closed, he said, "So what's your name, anyway?"

"Kathy. What's yours?"

"Derek. Call me Rick."

"You might not hate this summer as much as you think you're going to, Rick."

Rick slumped further down in his seat and didn't respond.

Kathy went back to her book. Maybe Rick was going to hate camp. He seemed pretty determined about it.

# TEN

"That's all you know about him?" Lia asked with dis-appointment.

"His name's Rick and he doesn't want to be at camp. End of story."

The Holiday Five had once again made themselves at home in Bunk Three. Lia and Jill, the more efficient members of the group, were unpacking and putting away their things in the rather rickety drawers the camp provided. Maddy had left her things tossed over her bed, while she struggled to pin a poster of a horse to the wall above it.

"Gee," Maddy said, "I know more about Beauty than you do about this guy." Beauty was the horse that

Maddy had ridden last year at camp. She was eagerly awaiting a chance to get reacquainted.

"Well, you've known Beauty longer, and she's probably more talkative," Kathy said. She was beginning to be a little tired of this topic.

Ellen Reiter, the bunk's counselor, came into the cabin. Ellen had been their counselor last year, too, and the girls were glad she had come back to camp and was in their bunk. Although Ellen could get mad at them when she had to—and she did have to—she was usually pretty nice. The only time she had really blown up last summer was when the girls had followed her and her boyfriend, another counselor, named Tommy Finelli, after lights-out.

Ellen glanced around the room. "There's a special campfire tonight, but all bags have to be unpacked before anyone can go. At this rate, you won't be ready until tomorrow night."

Erin and Kathy, who'd been lounging on their beds, groused a little, but got up and started digging into their bags.

"Say, Ellen, is Tommy back this summer?"

Ellen shook her head. "Nope. He decided to go to summer school."

"So you'll have to find somebody new," Jill said.

"Not this year. I don't want a boyfriend at camp. It's too hard when you don't see him again. When those Fourth of July fireworks start this year, I'm going to make sure that I'm not within one hundred feet of a guy."

"Well, I don't feel that way," Erin said, as soon as Ellen was out of earshot. "As a matter of fact, I want to go find Cal right now."

"You've barely started to unpack," Lia pointed out.

"Yeah. I guess I should get that done first." Then, looking like a whirling dervish, Erin began flinging clothes into drawers and putting shoes and jackets into the one large closet they all shared, and finally, with a flourish, she placed a photo of her family on the bureau.

"There," she said, almost out of breath. "I'm done."

"You can be amazing," Jill said drily.

"Aren't you glad I'm back?" Erin flashed her a smile.

"Where are you going to find Cal?" Maddy wanted to know. "You aren't going to his cabin, are you?"

"Well, why not?" Erin said, trying to sound nonchalant. Actually, she was a little nervous about meeting up with Cal. He had been on another bus, and it was only because she had seen him go into his bunk that she knew where to find him. She hadn't called to let him know she was going back to Wildwood because she'd wanted it to be a surprise. She hoped it was going to be a good one.

"You're going to walk into a cabin full of strange guys and ask for Cal?" Jill said. "Hey, bold, baby."

Erin checked herself out in the mirror. "Yeah, that's me." With a little wave, she went outside.

Camp Wildwood was set on a small lake, with the cabins and other buildings ringing the water. The boys' and girls' cabins were separated by the dining hall and other main buildings. Behind the cabins were the stables, and behind them were the woods where the campers went for overnights.

As she walked toward the end of the lake where Cal's cabin was, Erin breathed in the clean country air. Now that she was actually back at camp, Erin realized just how much she would have missed if she hadn't been able to return. Maybe she'd like to live in the country someday, she thought. There was something about being out in the middle of nowhere that calmed her. It was a feeling she wasn't used to.

Erin knew she should be planning what she was going to say to Cal. She thought back to the last time she had actually seen him, at Mrs. Tillman's holiday party. He had kissed her that night, and she hadn't told any of her friends about it. Then, she remembered how rude she had been to him the last time he called. Now she wished she had phoned and apologized or let him know about the scholarship. Somehow she had thought it would be more fun to just appear. Erin shook her head. Whatever had made her think surprising him was such a good idea?

Furtively, Erin walked over to the cabin. Now what? Erin had hoped that she'd just run into Cal outside his cabin, but no one was around. She didn't want to knock at the door, and she certainly didn't want to be caught peeking in the window. That would be great— Erin Moriarity, scholarship winner and camp pervert.

Erin felt foolish just standing there. After a few more minutes of wondering what she should do, she was ready to admit defeat and go back to Bunk Three. The girls would tease her, but that was better than being humiliated. Turning to go, Erin bumped right into the boy Kathy had sat next to on the bus: Rick.

"Oh, sorry," Erin mumbled, and tried to walk around him.

"Looking for somebody?"

"Not exactly."

"Either you are or you aren't."

"Okay, so I am."

Rick lifted an eyebrow. "Sassy."

"I want to see Cal Bennett. Do you know him?"

"Yeah, isn't he one of the slugs in there?" Rick asked, gesturing toward the cabin.

"Hey, just because you don't want to be here, don't take it out on everyone else," Erin retorted.

"How did you know I don't want to be here? Oh, I get it," Rick said, catching on. "You must be friends with that girl on the bus."

*Uh-oh,* Erin thought. *Now, I've gotten Kathy into trouble.*

"Girls," Rick said with disgust. Before he could go on, the cabin door opened, and Cal appeared.

"Erin!"

"I'm back after all," Erin replied, a little shakily.

"Well, I don't want to break up this romantic re-union," Rick said sarcastically. "I'll leave you love-birds to it."

Cal looked like he wanted to get into it with Rick, but Erin pulled him away. "He's an idiot. Forget about him."

"Okay," Cal said, smiling down at her.

"You're so tall," she said. "Even taller than you were at Christmas."

"And to think I started liking you because you were

one of the only girls at camp last summer who was
shorter than me."

"You're kidding! That was it?" Erin was a redhead
and could get mad fast.

"Yeah, I am. I would have liked you even if I was a
six-footer last summer. But what are you doing here?
After that last phone call . . ."

"I know, I know. It's a long story."

"Well, start talking," Cal said. "We've got the whole
summer."


The girls were headed to the opening-night cookout.
The younger children were having their own cookout
in a clearing in the woods, but the older kids were
going to the lakefront. After dinner, there was going to
be swimming and a game of nighttime volleyball.

"Are you going to eat with us," Jill asked Erin, "or
are you and Cal going to have dinner together?"

"Oh, I guess I'll let you have the honor of my presence," Erin said. "You got me here, I want to spend
some time with you."

"You were gone for an awfully long time this afternoon," Lia noted.

"And you didn't really tell us what went on," Maddy
added.

"And I'm not going to," Erin said firmly. After that obnoxious Rick had disappeared, Cal and she had taken a walk in the woods. She hadn't known that four in the afternoon could be such a romantic time.

A little wistfully, Maddy said, "It must be nice to have secrets like that."

When the girls got to the beach, the other kids had already gathered. Bunk Three dispersed to say hello to some of the campers they knew from last year. After a while, the counselors, with the help of some of the kids, got several fires going and began hauling out the boxes of hot dogs and buns, and marshmallows for toasting after the swim. Large coolers filled with ice and cans and cans of cola were being wheeled down in wagons.

As Kathy talked to a girl from Bunk Seven named Janice, she saw Rick standing alone by a tree. He wasn't wearing his usual angry expression. Not knowing he was being observed, he had let that drop, and what Kathy saw was a very good-looking boy who looked more unhappy than mad.

Kathy tried to keep her attention on Janice, but her eyes kept drifting back to Rick, who had by now gone over to the cooler and popped open a cola.

Janice followed Kathy's eyes. "So you saw him, too," Janice said knowingly. "He's pretty cute."

Kathy was embarrassed that she was being so obvious. Trying to be casual, though, she said, "Oh, I sat with him on the bus coming up."

"What did he say?" Janice asked eagerly.

"Not much." Kathy wasn't about to say anything else. Erin had already told her that Rick knew he had been a topic of discussion. Kathy didn't want any more conversations to get back to him. Saying there was someone else she wanted to say hello to, Kathy quickly moved away from Janice. She practically bumped into Erin and Cal.

"Hey," Erin said cheerfully, "the boys of Bunk Twelve want to eat dinner with the girls of Bunk Three."

"All the boys?" Kathy couldn't help asking.

"Well, not Rick Weller," Cal said.

So that's his last name, Kathy thought, Weller. "He doesn't like the girls of Bunk Three?"

"Or the boys of Bunk Twelve," Cal said.

But when it came time for the cookout to begin, Rick, to everyone's surprise, joined their circle. Not that he said anything. He silently ate his hot dog through all the talking and laughing, only speaking once—to ask for the mustard.

Kathy was glad that he was across the circle, not sitting next to her. But as the sun set and the only light came from the glow of the flames, she couldn't help thinking how attractive he looked in that shimmering light.

*Quit it,* she told herself. *This is ridiculous.* If she wanted to get interested in a guy at camp, there were plenty of them wandering around. What was the point of picking out the one boy who didn't want anything to do with Wildwood in general and her in particular?

She turned to the boy sitting next to her, Kenny, and said, "They're starting to organize teams for volley-ball. Wanna play?"

"Sure," Kenny said, perking up. He stood and pulled Kathy up by the hand. Out of the corner of her eye, she saw Rick taking notice. Together they ambled over to one of the nets.

Other kids had the same idea. Within a few minutes, almost everyone had divided into teams, and several vigorous games, filled with plenty of laughs and groans, were taking place.

Kathy played for a while, then realized that despite all the exertion, she was getting chilly. She decided to go back to the cabin and change from her thin tee into a more substantial sweatshirt.

After slipping into her shoes, Kathy walked off the beach toward the girls' cabin area. She went into Bunk Three, found her sweatshirt, and spent a moment looking at herself critically in the mirror. Her hair was all windblown, and a quick comb-through didn't help. Grabbing a barrette, she piled her hair on top of her head and clipped it. Maybe this wasn't her best look, but at least it would keep her hair out of her eyes.

It was dark, and Kathy was having a little trouble making her way back. She wished she were wearing sturdier shoes. In these soft moccasins she could feel every stone. She decided that instead of slipping on stones back to the lakefront, she'd go the longer way, along the sidewalk that led to the road. Her feet would thank her for it.

Kathy had just finished walking along the paved path and was about to turn down to the beach when she saw a figure standing out by the road, his thumb out to stop a passing car.

"You idiot!" Kathy muttered. "Rick, you're getting into real trouble now."

# ELEVEN

A dark car slowed down, and Rick walked toward the car. Running as fast as she could, Kathy yelled, "Don't, Rick!"

Rick turned to look at her, and the car picked up speed and swept past him. "You made me miss that ride," an exasperated Rick said.

"Then you ought to say thank you."

"What for?"

"Didn't you learn when you were about three that you shouldn't take rides with strangers?"

"I'm not three anymore. I can handle myself."

"Yeah, right." Kathy shook her head. "Don't you read the newspaper? It isn't only girls who can get in trouble doing things like getting into cars."

"I'll get a subscription when I get home," Rick said, turning away from her.

"Fine," Kathy said angrily. "I don't know what I'm doing out in the middle of the road trying to help someone who doesn't want to be helped anyway."

"Neither do I. Go back to the wienie roast."

Kathy started moving quickly away from the road, but in the dark she stumbled. "Oh!" she cried as she twisted her ankle.

Rick, who had flagged down another car, didn't hear her cry, but as he was about to get into the front seat, he saw Kathy struggling to get up. Reluctantly, he let the ride go and went over to help her. "I don't believe I missed another ride because of you," he said as he lifted her up by the elbow.

"Who asked you to stay?" Kathy asked through gritted teeth.

"You'd be lying here all night if I hadn't come back," Rick told her as she limped back toward the cabin, his arm around her waist.

"I wouldn't be here at all if I hadn't seen you doing something ridiculous."

For a second or two, they glared at each other. Then, Rick started to smile.

"What's so funny?" Kathy snapped.

"You. With your hair all pinned on the top of your head, you remind me of my grandmother."

For a second or two, Kathy thought she might slug him. But the silly grin on his face made her start laughing too. "All right, I'm not at my best."

"Still, for a grandmother, you don't look bad," Rick said.

Kathy felt a little tingle go down her back. All she said, though, was, "Do you think you can get me back to my cabin?"

"Want me to carry you?"

She didn't bother to answer that. "I'm in Bunk Three."

As they were approaching the bunk, Lia came out the door. She looked surprised to see Kathy and Rick together, and so close together at that. Then she noticed that Kathy was limping.

"What happened to you?"

"I . . . think I sprained my ankle. Rick found me and helped me back here."

Lia guessed that wasn't even half the story, but all she said was, "Do you want me to get Ellen?"

"No. Why don't we just go over to the infirmary and have the nurse look at my ankle."

With Rick on one side and Lia on the other, Kathy hobbled over to the infirmary. Rick didn't go in, though. He said to Lia, "Can you handle it from here?" When Lia nodded, he turned to leave.

"You're staying, right?" Kathy asked.

Rick nodded. "For now, anyway."

"Good."

"What was that all about?" Lia asked, confused. "He said he was staying, then he walked away."

"Oh, staying at camp," Kathy said vaguely. "You know he doesn't like it here."

Lia would have liked to know more, but now seeing to Kathy's foot took precedence. She'd find out the rest later.

Later, however, after the nurse had determined that Kathy had a minor sprain and ordered her to bed with an Ace bandage and an ice pack, Kathy didn't feel like talking. By then, her bunkmates had come back and wanted to know where Kathy had gone and how she had twisted her ankle. Kathy knew her friends would be fascinated by the story of Rick trying to run away from camp, but she felt a certain loyalty to him that kept her from telling what had happened.

So all she said was that she had gone back to get

her sweatshirt, she'd fallen, and Rick had found her. It felt odd not to be sharing everything with the girls, but somehow it didn't seem right to.

The next morning, Kathy was feeling much better.

"Do you want us to steal you something from the dining hall?"

"We're ready to pamper you," Jill said.

"No way. I'm not going to waste this beautiful day lounging around in bed." With that, she wobbled across to the dresser so she could get some clothes.

The dining hall was filled with kids by the time the girls got there.

"Sometimes I think we're crazy to wait in line for camp food," Lia said.

"Maybe it will be better this year," Kathy said, holding on to the wall to steady herself.

Erin shrugged. "I'm so happy to be here, I don't care what they feed me. I don't even mind working."

The girls were sitting down to hot cereal and milk—they had learned to avoid the scrambled eggs last summer—when Kathy saw Rick walk in. He saw her, too. He looked like he was going to turn away, but then he came over and gruffly asked, "How are you?"

"I'm much better, thanks."

Rick had to be aware that four other pairs of eyes were trained on him. "That's good," he said, and walked over to the food line.

"So what was Rick doing wandering around in the dark last night?" Maddy asked casually.

Kathy shrugged. "You'd have to ask him."

After breakfast it was time for the girls to separate for their various activities. Kathy was taking arts and crafts, while Maddy and Lia were horseback riding, and Erin and Jill were off for a swim.

Kathy was one of the first kids in the arts-and-crafts building. The counselor told her to get a pad of paper and a pencil. Other campers began filtering in, and one of them was Rick, who had his own pad under his arm.

It seemed silly not to go over to Rick, so that's what Kathy did. "You asked me how I was feeling this morning. I could ask you the same thing."

Rick sighed. He looked as vulnerable as he had last night before the campfire. "You were right. I admit it. Running away was stupid."

"So you'll stick it out here?"

"I don't have much choice."

Kathy felt relief. At least she didn't have to worry

about Rick doing anything like thumbing rides in the road again.

"Where were you going to go?" Kathy asked.

"Just home, I guess. Mrs. Tillman would have tracked down my parents eventually, and they would have sent me somewhere else, but at least I could have stayed there for a while. On the other hand, I don't have any money, so being at home might not have been all that much fun."

There were a lot more questions Kathy wanted to ask, but they were interrupted by a girl about eight with her hair in a ponytail who asked, "Is this the art class?"

Rick nodded politely but then he said, "Are you sure you're in the right place? Aren't you a little young?"

Kathy told him, "They mix up the ages. They think the older kids can help the younger kids."

The girl pointed to his obviously well-used pad. "Do you draw?"

"Yes."

"Can I see?"

Rick looked caught. The girl was so straightforward and appealing it was hard to turn her down.

"My name's Nancy," she offered, as though their

lack of introduction was what was keeping Rick from showing her his artwork.

Shrugging, he replied, "I guess you can see a few sketches." He flipped through the pad and found one of a collie. He showed it to Nancy.

"Is that your dog?"

"For now."

Before Nancy could ask what that meant, Kathy said, "You're really good, Rick."

He shrugged again, but he looked pleased. At Kathy's request, he showed them several more pictures, one a self-portrait, and another of a house. Kathy hadn't just been being nice. Rick really did have talent.

The drawing class passed quickly; Jerri, the arts-and-crafts counselor, had put several objects—including a baseball glove, a flower, and a piggy bank—on a table, and the kids were asked to draw any or all of them. It was something both the younger children and the older campers were able to do at their own level. Kathy thought her drawing was pretty good, but when she looked at Rick's piece, she saw his creativity as well as talent. He had drawn the glove holding the bank, with the flower sticking out of the pig's money slot. Jerri had smiled at Rick and patted him on the shoulder when she saw the drawing.

After the class, both Rick and Kathy were scheduled to go swimming, but a light rain was falling.

"What are we supposed to do now?" Rick asked.

"Anything we want. Go to the library, the game room, back to our bunks."

"What are you going to do?"

"I know what I'd like to do."

"Yeah, what's that?"

"Talk. The rec hall will be pretty noisy, but there's a back porch there," Kathy said, mustering her courage. She really did want to find out more about this boy.

"Okay."

Rick and Kathy ducked behind the rec hall and sat on the porch. The rain was falling more steadily now.

This was what Kathy had been waiting for, a chance to get to know Rick and find out what last night was all about. But now that they were alone together, Kathy didn't know how to begin. Finally, Rick started talking.

"About last night. I know it seemed weird, but I just wanted to get home."

"Because you don't like it here?"

"No. Because my home's not going to be around much longer."

"What do you mean?" Kathy asked.

"After my parents get home from their trip, we're moving." Rick's face darkened. "My dad got a job in Boston, and we're moving there at the end of the summer."

Kathy could see how upset Rick was over this. "You'll miss your friends."

"Yeah, I'll miss them. But it's really Corky I can't stand leaving."

"Who's Corky?"

Rick looked at her as if she should know. "My dog. That's who the drawings were of."

"Can't you take him with you?"

Rick shook his head. "We're going to live in an apartment where they don't allow dogs. Our next-door neighbors said they would take him. He's there now."

Kathy had never really had a pet, so she couldn't understand exactly how Rick was feeling. But she knew what it was like to change your life because of your parents' actions, and that's what she told him. Describing her fractured life split between her mother and her father, Kathy let Rick know he wasn't alone in parent roulette.

Rick was sympathetic. "What is it about parents? Don't they ever think that we might have lives, too?"

"They know that," Kathy said carefully, "but sometimes our lives clash with theirs."

"And they always win."

"Yeah, they do." Then Kathy thought about her father, and how he had really made an effort over the last months to understand her. "But they do their best, too, I think."

Rick sighed. "Yeah, I guess. My dad's a scientist, a medical researcher, and this new job will give him a chance to work on some important stuff."

"Would you want him to give that up?"

"I guess not." Rick smiled at her. "How did you get so smart?"

"Years of practice," Kathy said, smiling back.

"Maybe if I hang around with you all summer, I'll get smart, too. What do you think?"

"It's possible."


"Since we're sitting together at the fireworks, I guess that means I'm going to be spending the whole summer with you guys," Maddy said as she walked down to the beach with Lia and Jill.

"Hey, speak for yourself," Jill responded. "I'm not

done checking out all the boys. Just because the Fourth comes and goes doesn't mean we're going to be boy-less."

"I got a letter from Scott this afternoon," Lia said happily. "He really misses me."

"She won't be checking out the boys," Maddy told Jill.

"Uh-uh. And neither will Erin or Kathy," Jill added.

"No, they're already down there on the beach waiting for the fireworks." Lia pointed down to where Cal and Erin and Kathy and Rick were sharing a blanket.

Rick stretched out and looked up at the sky. "If I had known about this fireworks thing, I might not have been so down about coming to camp."

"Man, you were one obnoxious guy the first day or two," Cal said.

Rick just laughed. "I guess I was."

"I wasn't so sweet myself when I first got here last year," Erin said.

"Ancient history," Kathy told her. She turned to Rick. "If you stick around, maybe your behavior will become ancient history, too."

Dusk was falling. "So when do these fireworks start?" Rick asked.

"Not until it gets much darker," Kathy said. "You're not in a hurry are you?"

"Nope," Rick said with a smile.

Kathy leaned against him. "Me either."

Erin was totally content. "We don't have to rush anything. We've got a whole summer ahead of us."

# ABOUT THE AUTHOR

Ilene Cooper has been a children's librarian and a consultant for *ABC Afterschool Specials*. Currently, she is the children's book review editor for *Booklist*. Among her popular series are *Hollywood Wars* and *The Kids from Kennedy Middle School*, and she is the author of the young adult novel *Starring Buddy Love*. She lives in Highland Park, Illinois.

Level 5.0
Points 4